When I Get Older
I'll Understand

Barbara Bailey

ISBN 1-56315-211-8

Young Adult Fiction
© Copyright 2000 Barbara Bailey
All rights reserved
First Printing—2000
LOC 99-64515

Request for information should be addressed to:

SterlingHouse Publisher
The Sterling Building
440 Friday Road
Pittsburgh, PA 15209
www.sterlinghousepublisher.com

Cover design: Michelle Vennare - SterlingHouse Publisher
Photography: Michelle Burton-Brown - SterlingHouse Publisher
Typesetting: McBeth Typesetting and Design
Models: Sha'Rhonda Brandon, Jackie Rice,
Sparkle Graham, Parese Carter

Printed in Canada

Young girl, tempest tossed

Young girl, never lost

b bailey

Chapter 1

Joan's mother and father were at odds again. Joan's father was saying, "but we don't need to move." However, this time there was less force behind his words.

Joan's mother countered with her usual argument. "Joan'll be dating soon and it'll be wonderful if she's able to go out with boys from the really good families. And 'those boys from around here' won't travel to the west side to see Joan."

Joan's mother added, as she always did whenever they spoke of moving, "Joan should have a home, a real home, not merely an apartment, to entertain her friends. And it'll be good for all of us to have enough room to have a study at the very least. We really do need more space."

"Those boys," her mother mentioned, preferred not to recognize the existence of Chicago's west side. It was a no man's land. The right people her mother was talking about did not live there because they could afford to live elsewhere. Joan's mother wanted the family to live where these people lived.   She wanted to move to Chicago's south side.

Joan was a bright, sensitive girl of nearly four-teen. She was in the eighth grade and looking for-ward to high school. She knew her mother want-ed to move because of the opportunities for Joan to meet the "right people."

Joan's parents were professional people, a title they liked to use. Both were educators, another term they enjoyed. Her mother taught third grade at a nearby elementary school and her father was an assistant principal at a west side high school. Joan and her younger sister, Betsy, lived in a west side apartment building with their parents.

Joan, like her father, did not feel the need to move. She had enough friends here. There was Marie who lived in the same apartment building and walked to and from school with Joan. Whenever Joan wanted to go to a Saturday movie matinee, Marie was always available. True, Joan paid both fares, but they had fun. Marie was defi-nitely a friend.

Janene was another good friend and classmate who shared lunches and secrets. Joan often gave part of her lunch to Janene, who never seemed to have enough in her lunch bag even for herself. In turn, Joan learned every "secret" Janene knew. And she knew plenty. She knew which boys the eighth grade girls liked. She knew how much her classmates received in allowances. She even knew where Karen Smith, also an eighth grader and the prettiest girl in school, bought her clothes, despite what the labels said. In short, Janene knew everything.

Joan could even count some of the boys among her friends. There was Alphonzo Rubin. He was a patrol boy and she saw him every day. They always said, "Hi," to each other. Joan thought he was really special. He was tall, dark, and — Alphonzo Rubin was tall and dark. Joan was sure that he was not one of the boys her mother would select as suitable. She was not able to say exactly why she felt that her mother would disapprove of Alphonzo Rubin. Joan thought there was more involved than just the wrong address.

If they did move, Joan realized that her parents would have to spend more time traveling to work. Joan did not think it necessary to take sides. The issue would resolve itself without any help from her. It was just a matter of time. Either her father would give in, or her mother would give up. After all, it was still fairly early in the school year. Another issue would soon replace this one. Joan decided not to pay too much attention to what her parents had to say about moving.

Joan was lucky she could talk to both parents, but conversations with her mother were not the same as those with her dad. Her mother only seemed to hear what others were saying. Joan had discovered some time ago that her mother only heard what reinforced her own ideas of how things were. Discordant views were dealt with much as a shut window keeps out a chilling wind. But Joan's father was open and receptive to her opinion. Though he might not agree with what she said, he was a real listener. Not long ago she and her father had discussed something that had been bothering her. The two of them were driving in the family car when Joan asked about the "right people."

"Dad, what exactly does Mother mean when she says 'the right people'?"

"She's talking about people who have values and aspirations," was his reply.

"Mother's always saying that we should be careful to only associate with the right people. Aren't we the right people?"

"Certainly we are. We have firm and definite values and we want to keep moving up in the world. We don't want to stagnate, that is, we want to advance socially, economically, and educationally. And of course, we want the best for you." Her father paused and then laughed. "I'm beginning to sound like a principal, aren't I?"

"Oh, no, Dad, you aren't at all. I thought I knew what Mother meant, but she is always going on about it."

"Don't exaggerate, Joan. She does bring the subject up, but there's usually a good reason. She's concerned about impressions and appearances. But most of all, she's concerned about what's best for you."

"I suppose I knew that all along, but it sounds clearer coming from you."

Joan glanced at her father.   He was smiling, pleased he had made her happy. Their ride continued in pensive silence.

Pushing all thoughts of moving from her mind, Joan continued to live each day as she always had. There was school during the week and time for her friends, Janene and Marie. Joan thought she'd like to be a teacher when she grew up and played school with her friends whenever she could. One Thursday afternoon the three girls were in their usual spot in the vestibule of Joan's building. On the hard floor Janene and Marie sat on their coats as Joan stood in front of them, pretending to be the teacher, and started to explain the math homework.

"Joan, I mean, Miss Williams, I can't seem to do this problem. You make it sound easy, but when I try, I get stuck," moaned Janene, mainly out of embarrassment at not being able to solve the problem.

"Me too. It makes sense when you say it, but I can't do it on my own," Marie chimed in.

Joan bent down to look at the work the girls were doing and almost in a flash saw their dilemma. They were trying to divide mixed numbers. "You're forgetting to invert the second fraction. That's why your answers aren't coming out right. If you write out all the steps, then you'll remember to invert. Remember to show all your work. Here, let me do one for you. I always circle the second fraction to remind me to invert it." As Joan demonstrated the next problem she was thinking that this was a very basic concept the girls should have mastered long ago. *Maybe they're just pretending to make mistakes so the play will be more realistic*, she thought. She hoped that was the case. They were all planning to take algebra in high school in September.

Marie and Janene looked on and seemed to follow along as they watched Joan write down the fractions and lightly circle the one to be inverted. "Now, you try the next on your own and I'll watch," said Joan in her best imitation of their math teacher's nasal voice.

Both Marie and Janene were successful this time and in no time the homework was finished. They also finished the more complicated work with decimals and equations. All three girls knew their work was one hundred percent correct.

"Joan," said Janene, "I'm really glad you can help us so much. I wish I was smart like you and that my parents had gone to college. My mom and dad can't help me with anything but the simplist work and that's not usually where I need help. And it's really too bad your dad isn't a principal. He's smart and he's nice, but he's..." Janene came to an abrupt stop as her face reddened. Her complexion was too light a shade of brown for her to hide the blush.

"What were you going to say?"

"Don't take this the wrong way, it's just that colored men just don't seem to make it to the top around here. My dad's always saying what a shame it is that people still look and judge by skin color and race. He says you'd think people who live in the North would have gotten over that. He says even colored people judge other colored people by skin color." Then Janene sang a playground ditty, "'If you're white, you're alright; if you're brown, stick around; if you're black, get back.' But what can he do? He can't change anything. He's just one person. At least I don't choose my friends because of their color like Karen Smith does. Karen won't even play with me because some of my friends are 'too brown' according to her. I think she thinks she's white because she's so light. I know she's stuck-up."

"Oh, don't be silly," said Joan. "What could the color of anyone's skin have to do with anything? That doesn't make sense. There must be other reasons." Joan was not using her teacher voice now.

Joan knew this was something she would have to talk about with her dad. Surely Janene couldn't be right. Joan knew her dad was smart and it was just a matter of time before he was promoted and got his own school. *Isn't it?* she thought. She had not been concerned about her own dark skin. That is, until now she had not been concerned. She had friends and she was smart. That was enough.

After hearing what Janene said, Joan could not help but look at things a bit differently. When she watched television in the evenings, she now realized that the shows they watched were about white families. *Father Knows Best* and *Leave It to Beaver* were favorites, but there were not any colored people in them. Even her afternoon program, *American Bandstand*, had white teen dancers. Only *The Nat King Cole Show* had a host that looked like someone in her family. Nat King Cole looked more like her and her father than anyone else they saw on television. Then she began to think about the movies she and Marie went to on Saturdays. *A Summer Place*, starring Troy Donahue and Sandra Dee, was popular. Troy Donahue was the current teen heart throb. He was tall and blond as were many of the other teen idols. *Where were all the colored actors? Where were all the colored movies?* Joan wondered. She could only think of two male actors that fit, Harry Bellafonte and Sidney Portier. Without even thinking hard, she could list a dozen white actors she and her girlfriends liked to watch: Tony Curtis, Rock Hudson, Tab Hunter, Robert Stack, Robert Mitchum, Cary Grant, John Wayne, Russ Tamblyn, Van Johnson, Sal Mineo, James Dean, and Montgomery Cliff popped immediately to mind. In fact, she could have named many more than a dozen. Even the music seemed white now that she thought about it. This new rock and roll singer, this Elvis Presley, the radio stations were playing was a prime example. What about the ones she liked to listen to? What about Chuck Berry and Fats Domino and Sam Cooke? Joan listened to them on WVON, yet they were hardly getting the attention she thought they deserved. Yes, she must talk to her father.

Rounding out her week was church on Sunday followed by a ride around the city. The family attended a church not too far from their apartment. Joan did not listen carefully to the sermons and found them overly long. If you did not go to church on Sunday, you did not do anything else on Sunday either. It had been that way for as long as she could remember.

Even with routines still in place, Joan knew the moving issue had not disappeared, because her parents still talked about it regularly. The more her father reasoned that they did not have to move, the more her mother said they did. A storm was gathering and Joan had no desire to be caught in it. If Betsy were older, the two of them could console one another as they waited out the storm. But Betsy, who was only six, was still a baby in Joan's eyes. Joan could not expect much comfort from her. She probably was not even aware that anything unusual was happening. If they did move, Joan would be uprooted. She would have to make new friends. She did not easily make friends with boys and girls her own age.

Chapter 2

One snowy January afternoon, Joan returned from school to find her mother entertaining a guest over cocktails. Normally Joan would have stayed after school an extra hour to work in the library. Today there was no work for her, so she came straight home.

This must be a very important occasion. Joan could not recall her mother ever having a white woman in the house and liquor was never served until after 7 p.m. Her mother had strict notions about propriety. When Joan looked at the two women in the living room light, she realized, not for the first time, how different she and her mother were. Her mother was bubbly, beautiful, and almost looked as though she were white. Joan had not given that last part much thought. Her mother was her mother. They were family and that was that. Joan, on the other hand, was definitely brown-skinned, though not as dark as her father. But even he seemed to pull people towards him. He had a wonderful personality and a winning smile. In some ways, Joan was not like either of her parents.

"Joan," Mrs. Williams practically cooed. "Please come in and meet Miss Thomas. She's the school counselor."

Joan responded by immediately entering the living room and greeting the visitor. Joan was quite comfortable around adults. "Hello, Miss Thomas, I'm very glad to meet you. Do you work at Mother's school?"

"No, Joan. Your mother and I don't work at the same school. I'm one of the guidance counselors at Hyde Park High School."

Joan's mother giggled uncharacteristically, letting Joan know at once she was privy to some information her mother was not yet ready to share.

"Oh," said Joan as she finished removing her camel-colored Chesterfield school coat. "If you're talking about high school, may I stay?" she asked in her most charming voice.

Joan's mother realized that she had temporarily lost control of the situation. She would rectify that before long. Now she had to concentrate on the scene as it was being played.

"Joan," said her mother, recovering her aplomb, "I would very much like for you to join us. I was just saying to Vera that it was too bad you weren't here so that we could get your views on where to attend high school."

As if on cue the blond woman added, "One of the most important decisions you'll ever make is what high school to attend. Every girl isn't lucky enough to have a choice or to have parents who are willing to make a sacrifice for her. At Hyde Park we can offer you a solid college preparatory program and we can, with your full cooperation, get you into one of the really good colleges after graduation. A smart young lady like you should do very well."

Joan knew the arguments about the right people her mother was constantly spouting. Now Joan's vanity had been appealed to. She had missed none of what Miss Thomas had implied. Why shouldn't a girl as bright as she be groomed for a really good college? Surely that was more important than dating any boy at this time. Joan sat down near her mother's friend. Joan smiled, nodded, and paid close attention as Miss Thomas continued. Like a sponge, Joan absorbed every word. She listed to Miss Thomas talk about foreign language labs, accelerated math and English classes, modern science facilities. Miss Thomas recounted academic praises that the faculty had received. But most of all she soaked in the information about the integrated student body. Here was an opportunity to learn with people from different racial and ethnic backgrounds. Her neighborhood high school would be just like her current elementary school. Everyone was pretty much the same. Complexions might vary, but all the students were colored, or as some of her teachers proudly said, they were Negroes.

Joan had studied about the segregated South. Only a few years ago *Brown versus The Board of*

Education settled the issue of separate public schools for white and colored children. The Supreme Court ruled that schools for colored students exclusively were not equal to white schools. The educational opportunities offered at the colored schools were inferior. The practice of segregated schools was unconstitutional. Yet Joan's school had not changed. Her school as well as her neighborhood was bland. All of these thoughts made Joan feel as though she had been through the looking glass. Reentering her own world where everyone was the same would not be easy. She spent the rest of the week with Miss Thomas' words uppermost in her thoughts.

The following Sunday Joan and her family took their usual rambling ride around the city. The snow covered lawns of the north side's Gold Coast were a blur to Joan. Her little sister's prattle about the icicle-laden trees that covered Beverly Hills, one of the far south side's affluent residential areas, fell on deaf ears. Joan could hardly wait for them to arrive in Hyde Park, which they would pass on their route home. She had been there many times before, but she had never actually seen Hyde Park. Before, it had been just another area of this very large city. Now it was more than that because Hyde Park High School was there. On this trip Joan intended to look carefully.

"Clarence, it's almost dark," Joan's mother said. "Perhaps we should start home and ..."

"No," Joan blurted out too loudly as she was jolted out of her reverie by the thought of not seeing Hyde Park. Then more quietly she added, "If we take the Outer Drive, we can be there very quickly. We don't have to spend too much time sightseeing."

Mr. Williams looked at his daughter through the car's rear view mirror. She gave him a quick wink, unaware of the smile that visited her mother's face. In a few minutes, her father turned the station wagon onto the Drive and headed north. Lake Michigan, which was on their right as they traveled east on the Outer Drive, was frozen and snow covered. The wind gusted furiously and rocked the car. Soon they made a left turn from the Outer Drive. The wind died down, and almost at once, looming in front of Joan was Hyde Park High School.

"Dad, can we drive around the school?"

Hyde Park High School was larger and more impressive-looking than Joan had previously remembered. There were fine columns flanking the entranceways of this great stone structure. Not a single window was boarded shut. No glass bottles littered the landscape. The school was gigantic, gleaming, and inviting. It was a stark contrast to the west side high school located in her neighborhood.

In her mind Joan walked up and down what must be tiled corridors. She heard the rapid thump, thump, thump of a basketball in a real gym, not a converted cafeteria, as boys perfected their skills. She climbed a stairway to reach another level and walked up a hallway. Peering into one room she saw students working advanced algebraic equations. Opening the door of another classroom, she heard students responding in unison, *"Ich spreche deutch."* From yet another classroom Joan overheard a teacher discussing the character of Pip in *Great Expectations*. That was one of her favorites. She could understand his feelings. She knew what it was to want to please so badly that it hurt. It sometimes seemed to her that she had been trying to please her mother all of her life.

Splat! A large snowball hit the side of their car. Joan's daydream melted just like the snowball when it reached the warm window of their station wagon.

"Have you seen enough, Joan?" her father inquired. "After all, there's only so much you can learn from the outside of a school."

"Joan, do you remember Miss Thomas?" her mother asked. "I'm sure she can arrange a visit for you, if you're interested in seeing more, that is."

Joan was learning to play her mother's game. In fact, she now felt that she, not her mother, manipulated some of the moves. "Yes, Mother, I think now I'm ready to see the school."

Joan's father had not missed a thing. His wife had done it again, he reflected. Joan would soon begin to think that attending Hyde Park High had been her own idea. *At least it's not a bad choice*, thought her father. What he said was, "It's almost dark. Let's head home."

Joan watched as the school receded in the distance. Her father turned the car east toward Lake Michigan and then north as they again picked up the Outer Drive. Soon they headed west and before long they were home.

Chapter 3

Exactly one week had passed since the family drive to Hyde Park High School. It was Sunday and Joan awakened to sounds coming from the kitchen. Joan's bedroom was next to the living room, which was a comfortable but open area.

Voices easily drifted from the kitchen and through the living room to her ears because there were no doors to block the sounds. Joan rarely even shut the door to her bedroom, which she shared with Betsy.

Sitting up in bed, Joan listened as her parents' conversation confirmed what she had suspected all week. The moving issue was not dead.

Joan heard Betsy stir as she rolled over in her twin bed. Between their two beds was a night-stand that was supposed to act as a room divider. But how, Joan wondered, *do you divide a too small room effectively?* Only when Betsy was sound asleep did Joan feel that any part of the room was solely hers. Even that was sometimes spoiled by her having to leave the door open because Betsy did not like to have it closed. It scared her, Betsy said, to have the door shut.

Betsy turned again, stretched, and then got out of bed. Joan did not want her sister to think that she had been listening to their parents' conversation. So she said, almost before Betsy's feet touched the carpet, "Morning, Betsy. Looks like we woke up at the same time today." Betsy, who was not an early morning talker, had no reply.

The sound of Joan's parents' voices was replaced by the aroma of Sunday breakfast. Pancakes, bacon, eggs, and grits, Joan guessed from the scents. Over them all was the special fragrance of freshly perked coffee. *Sundays are great*, Joan thought.

That good feeling about Sundays was a recent development. Previous Sundays had been all downhill for her after breakfast. Once the leisurely meal had been completed, they would hurry to get ready for church. After a too long sermon would come the even longer Sunday drive. Today, however, Joan was anxious to get to church because it meant the ride would be next.

Sitting down to breakfast, Joan heard her father say, "Take all the time you want this morning. We aren't going to church."

Joan felt as though her world had come to an end. She was shattered. How would she ever get through this day? More immediately, how would she swallow the forkful of pancakes she had just put in her mouth? Deciding to wash it down with orange juice, she ventured to ask timidly, "Why aren't we going to church? Is someone sick?" Illness and extremely bad weather had been the only excuses allowed for missing church. Joan knew the day was clear, though perhaps a little cold.

Her parents exchanged glances. Joan thought she saw her mother incline her head towards her husband. Before Joan had time to reflect further, her father answered her question.

"We thought we'd do something different today."

Joan did not hear the rest of the response. She was too busy thinking that today of all days her parents had decided to do something else. Years of predictability were broken like the china saucer from a childhood tea set, each fragment representing a separate and precious memory. Caught up in introspection, Joan was oblivious to her real world.

When Joan did not show any interest in the comments, her father guessed that his daughter's mind was elsewhere. Touching her gently on the shoulder he said, "I thought you'd be pleased. What's the matter?"

Brought back to reality, Joan could only stare at her father as she managed a weak, "I'm sorry. What did you say? I was thinking of something else while you were talking."

"I said, I thought we'd do something different today, like go to a realtor's office and see some homes in Hyde Park.. But if this isn't a good day for you, I'm sure we can ..."

Joan leaped up from the table and threw her arms around her dad's neck before he could finish the sentence or change his mind. "Oh, Daddy, Daddy! Of course we can miss church," she said excitedly, and then added more quietly, "just this once," as she regained her composure.

Joan could hardly wait to be off and had already pushed her chair back from the table when Betsy asked, "May I have some more pantakes, please?"

Usually everyone laughed when Betsy said "pantakes" instead of pancakes. This morning, Joan did not find it at all amusing. She did not share her parents' laughter. Because they always ate together as a family, Joan knew that she could not leave the table until her sister had finished eating. Eating as a family also had to do with her mother's sense of propriety.

Finally Betsy completed her pancakes and Joan's parents finished their second cups of coffee. The dishes were cleared from the table, rinsed, and neatly stacked for a later washing. *At least mother didn't insist on washing them before going house hunting*, thought Joan. After putting on their Sunday best, they all got in their station wagon and proceeded directly to Hyde Park. There was no circuitous route today, but a straight path instead.

The drive was a blur. There were just tones of gray and white from the buildings they passed and an occasional flash of color from a brightly colored car. It seemed an eternity, but finally they arrived at the realtor's. A rotund but dapperly dressed agent named Mr. Zimmermann met the family. After introductions were accomplished, Mr. Zimmermann suggested they ride in his Cadillac "to view the properties" as he phrased it. Joan's father and the agent rode in the front of the black auto while Joan, Betsy, and their mother took seats in the back.

Mr. Zimmermann said he had selected three houses and one apartment for them to see. Bus transportation was conveniently located near each and each house had its unique selling points. As they drove, the name of the streets rang melodically in Joan's ears as she whispered them from street signs: Drexel, Ingleside, Greenwood, Kenwood, Blackstone. All of these and more were to be found in a relatively compact area bounded between Lake Michigan and the Outer Drive on the east and Cottage Grove Avenue on the west. No one even called it the south side of Chicago without being careful to include the magical words "Hyde Park" that designated this neighborhood.

Mr. Zimmermann pulled his Cadillac in front of a great, graystone mansion. No other words described it. Its stone reminded Joan of the material castles were made of. The house was gigantic. The glass windows glistened as the sunlight bounced off of them. The building and grounds seemed to take up nearly a quarter of a city block.

Joan could not suppress the "Wow!" that escaped from her innermost self. Her mother, on the other hand, heaved a sigh. A sigh of what, Joan could not quite tell.

The house stood like an empty castle. The occupants had left no traces of themselves. That did not stop Joan from imagining what must have gone on in the house as they walked through its many rooms. The first floor included a parlor. It was here, Joan was convinced, that the lady of the house planned her many charitable activities over tea with a few close friends. The living room had a wood-burning fireplace around which many family fireside chats had no doubt taken place. The kitchen held little attraction for Joan, so she let her imagination turn itself loose as they passed into the formal dining room.

Joan continued letting scenes play themselves out in her mind. Beneath crystal chandeliers the husband and wife must have discussed politics, economics, and literature as the children listened attentively while eating a finely prepared meal. Joan's imagination did not have room to consider the cook, or the maid, or other household staff that must have been employed to keep everything running smoothly. Instead she next focused her imagination on the five large bedrooms on the second floor. But most of all she was dazzled by the ballroom on the third floor. It covered the entire top floor of the house. She was certain that it was used for the many wonderful parties given by the family she created in her mind.

"Can you imagine it!" she said to her mother in awed tones. "A private ballroom! These people must have been really rich."

"Yes," her mother said. "They certainly must have been." To Mr. Zimmermann she said, "This is really lovely, but let's not make up our minds without seeing the other houses." With that she closed the heavy mahogany double doors of the ballroom. A hollow thud was heard, followed by the echo of footsteps as they descended the wooden stairs.

The next house was not nearly as grand as the first. Its special feature was that it faced a park that would boast beautiful flowers throughout the spring and summer months. The house was well-maintained and more than adequate for their needs, but Joan's imagination did not feel as free in this house. She was not superstitious, but she did not feel happy in this house. *Maybe something tragic happened here. Maybe....* But her musings were interrupted by her father's statement to the agent. "This, too, is a sound house, but one can't be too hasty about major decisions."

The third house was a total disappointment. It was what in real estate language would be termed cozy. In Joan's language the house was tiny. Its special feature was simply a Hyde Park address. Her parents, always polite, walked through the house, listening to what Mr. Zimmermann said on its behalf. It was Betsy who, not yet schooled in social graces, said aloud what each was thinking. "This house is little. It's like where we live now."

Knowing glances were exchanged among the other members of the Williams family. Joan's father said without much enthusiasm, "Let's see the last place. We don't have to decide today, but we might as well see everything that Mr. Zimmermann lined up."

Joan's exasperation was difficult to conceal. She knew they had come to look at houses. This next place was an apartment, a flat. *Why waste time looking at it*, she thought. Always the trooper, she put on a smile and said brightly, "Might as well look."

The Williams family again piled into Mr. Zimmermann's Cadillac and headed toward Hyde Park Boulevard. The tree-lined street that would be resplendent with greenery and filled with people in the spring was quiet. The bare trees were wearing winter white with an occasional diamond-like gleam from an icicle. The trees looked like sentries guarding the brownstone apartment buildings that were on either side of the tree-lined boulevard. Because there were only a few cars parked on the street, Mr. Zimmermann was able to pull up directly in front of the address he wanted.

Unlike most of the other buildings on the Boulevard, this one was made of gray stone. It had three stories. The apartment they were to look at was on the second floor. Joan's parents were first to follow the agent into the vestibule. Joan and Betsy brought up the rear. Joan noticed how heavy the beveled glass entry door was when she caught it to keep it from closing on her and Betsy. The white marble floor and ornate wall tiles were next to catch her eye. On either side of the entryway were gold-colored mailboxes. There were three on each side. All except one were labeled carefully with Old English characters. Joan thought about how her family name would look in the rectangular space. Four marble steps led up to another beveled glass door. Behind it were thickly carpeted stairs and a heavily polished mahogany banister.

Up the stairs they climbed in silence until reaching apartment 2A. Another heavy mahogany door, this one with bronze nameplate and lion-shaped knocker, greeted them. There was also a buzzer and an intercom system inconspicuously recessed into the wall to the right of the door.

The real estate agent opened the door with a key and admitted the Williamses one by one. There was a long, wide corridor with many half-opened doors just to the left of the foyer.   To Joan's immediate right was a huge living room that overlooked Hyde Park Boulevard. Farther back from the living room, but also getting its light from the Boulevard, was the solarium.

Joan wanted to explore the hallway, but Mr. Zimmermann was ushering them into the living room. "Mrs.Williams," he was saying. "the parquet floors are beautiful enough to remain as they are or they can be adorned with oriental carpets. The fireplace you see is a real wood-burning one; and there's another in the master bedroom."

"Really," replied Joan's mother without much animation in her voice.

"In the spring when the trees are in full bloom, you'll have a magnificent view from these bay windows," Mr. Zimmermann continued.

"Indeed," said Joan's mother in the same lackluster way.

Their eyes were next directed to massive dark wooden sliding doors. Upon pushing them aside, they discovered a partially mirrored, partially wallpapered room complete with chandelier. Once again the north windows looked over the Boulevard. The parquet floors here, as in the living room, appeared to be waiting for a fine oriental rug. *Surely*, thought Joan, *Mother wouldn't cover this beautiful floor with wall-to-wall carpeting*.

"Now for the solarium ...." But Joan did not hear what else the agent said for she was eyeing the long corridor with its doors ajar, longing to see what was behind each.

Finally everyone moved from the solarium and headed toward the corridor. The first room off to the right was the kitchen. There was a narrow, tiled passage that led from it to the dining room. This was a most interesting feature to Joan. It reminded her of the hidden passage in the romantic novels she sometimes read.

"Isn't that a bit awkward?" commented Joan's mother about the tiled walkway.

The agent replied that the previous occupants probably had domestic help, so that was not really a problem for the lady of the house. Changing the subject, the real estate man talked about the room opposite the kitchen. He suggested possible uses for a room of its generous size.

Joan's mother knew very well what the space was for. She was referring to the narrowness of the passage, not the function of the rooms to which it led. Mr. Zimmermann, however, could not know that.

"Or perhaps a library or a study," added Joan's father, making a rare comment about the apartment.

Farther down the corridor was the master bedroom, complete with wood-burning fireplace. There were two additional bedrooms of more than ample proportions with a bathroom adjoining each. Joan, however, could not dismiss the curious arrangement of smaller rooms that were accessed by the narrow, tiled passage.

Joan knew she should be quiet when adults were discussing business matters, but she really wanted to inquire about those rooms. When she could no longer contain her curiosity she asked, "What were those smaller rooms used for, Mr. Zimmermann?"

"They were the maid's quarters. In Hyde Park it's quite fashionable to have a live-in domestic," was the pronouncement.

Before any of the others could respond, Joan's father quickly interjected, as any man whose ancestors were slaves would, "we can find some other perfectly good use for those rooms."

"Daddy, does that mean we're going to buy this apartment?" asked Betsy, who found Joan's curiosity contagious.

"It doesn't mean that at all. It simply means that a good use could be made of those rooms." After saying that, Joan's father began a close inspection of the walls, the baseboards, the door hinges, the tiles, and the like, making little "hums" and "ahs" as he did. No one dared interrupt him.

At last he said, "There's a good bit of work that needs to be done before a family could move in." With that he began to point out defects to Mr. Zimmermann. There was a crack in the plaster here; a tile was chipped there; there were some stains on the marble basins in the bathrooms; the water pipes in the kitchen seemed to need replacing. The list appeared endless. All the while that Joan's father talked, Mr. Zimmermann wrote. Then Joan's dad asked his wife if she noticed anything that he may have missed.

"No, dear. I think you covered everything. I guess with all that needs to be done, we might as well continue our search. This place will never be ready as soon as we need it. We can look some more next weekend," Joan's mother concluded.

Joan almost blurted out that even with all of the defects her father had pointed out, this place was much better than where they now lived. But Joan was wary of entering the conversation at this point. She had risked enough by asking about the strange rooms. Betsy, taking a cue from her sister's silence, also said nothing.

Mr. Zimmermann suggested they go to his office and finish up for the day. "We can decide on some properties to look at next week. The girls can watch TV. I have one in the office."

Once more the Williamses got in the realtor's large car. Before long they arrived at the building that housed his office. Joan and Betsy were settled comfortably in front of a small television set. Their parents went into an inner office with Mr. Zimmermann.

Joan could hardly keep her mind on the Western that had been turned on for their enjoyment. She wanted to be in the room with her parents. She wanted to know what they were talking about. She felt old enough to be included in something this important. Betsy, on the other hand, was totally absorbed by the TV program.

After what seemed like forever, Joan's parents emerged from the office. There were handshakes of departure. Within a few minutes, Joan and Betsy were seated in the station wagon for the trip home. The silence in the car was oppressive. Mr.

Williams turned around, looked at both girls, but directed his comments to Joan. "We took it."

"The apartment -it's ours?" stammered Joan.

"Yes," this time her mother continued and smiled as she spoke. "It'll mean a big sacrifice, but it'll be worth it. We may not be able to buy our oriental carpets at Marshall Field's, but we'll manage."

Joan was both elated and saddened. She was happy about the larger place to live in and having her very own bedroom, but she was unhappy at the thought of having to make new friends. She had a feeling that when they moved from their current neighborhood, the connections with the people there would end. Janene, Marie, and Alphonzo Rubin would have no place in her new life. In fact, if her mother had her way, there would be no room for the people she now called friends.

Joan recalled overhearing a phone conversation between her mother and one of their neighbors. Joan's mom was saying that she thought it ridiculous that Nancy Tipple used the last name of the father of each of her children instead of using her own last name. Mrs. Tipple had three sons and none of them shared her own last name. Joan had never seen Mr. Tipple, but she assumed there was one until she heard her mother's remarks. It was probably this aspect of Mrs. Tipple that Joan's mother objected to. *If mother knew Alphonzo Rubin, she would think he was a nice boy. He can't help what his mother's like.*

Janene and Marie were not nearly as smart as Joan. She guessed that was why her mother didn't really care for them. Joan knew her mother approved of Karen Smith. There were always comments about how well she dressed and how neatly she wore her long, brown hair, in two thick braids with bangs that had a hint of a wave to them. In many ways, Karen reminded Joan of her little sister. Karen, however, would not play with Joan. In fact, Karen only spoke to Joan when adults were present. Otherwise, Joan didn't seem to exist for Karen. Joan wondered if what Janene had said about Karen could be true. *Am I too brown to be her friend?*

The next months were a blur. Not only was there the move to be concerned with, but there was also Joan's graduation from elementary school. The guide sheet from Joan's school said all girls were to dress in white, below-the-knee party dresses for the ceremony. Joan preferred a soft pastel shade to complement her rich brown coloring. White was too stark in her opinion. Joan's mother, whose light coloring accounted for her nickname, Kitty; her complexion reminded people of a tawny feline, was not expected to be sympathetic. To Joan's dismay, a white dress without any hint of color was chosen.

Graduation day and moving day were a week apart. Joan, who was at the top of her class, had earned the honor of delivering the valedictory address. Her speech was excellently prepared, for she had worked long and hard on it. Her greatest thrill came when her classmates refused to believe that she, not her faculty advisor, composed it.

"...*The specter of nuclear annihilation is no longer a phantasm. It is a reality. We have witnessed the awful destructive power of the atomic bomb. We have witnessed man's inhumanity to man. But we, of this graduating class, have power, too. We must make it our task to use our power, our brain power, to counteract the forces that would destroy us all. We can be, and we will be successful....*" The audience applauded enthusiastically when Joan completed her speech.

After the graduation ceremony, Joan's only wish was to rush home and get out of her dress. Her parents had other plans. To celebrate this milestone, they all went to the Tropical Hut, a very popular restaurant on the south side that specialized in seafood. The large open dining area was decorated in an island motif and had a welcoming ambience. Joan, however, was preoccupied with thoughts of changing out of her stark white dress that made her look as dark as she felt. She ate her shrimp dinner, but did not really taste it. Her parents, caught up in the celebration, failed to notice how sullen Joan was. The first thing Joan did when she got home was to remove her depressingly white dress. In her hurry to take it off, she tore an ugly hole in the bodice. "It really was an accident," she later explained to her mother. Yet Joan was happy about never having to wear that dress again. Her mother wisely made no comment.

The following week Joan and her mother made several trips to stores to start stocking the new apartment. Their lease began on the first of June, although they did not move in then. Joan's father persuaded the realtor to let him sign a long-term rental agreement. Therefore, the apartment remained available for them those few extra weeks at no additional expense. At the end of June the Williames were ready to make the break with west side living and become Hyde Parkers.

Chapter 4

During the summer, Joan found the chance to talk to her father about what Janene had said a couple of months earlier about the color of one's skin being a key factor in success. Though Joan and her dad did not ride together as often as they had when they lived on the west side, she still enjoyed the private time spent with him. One evening he was going to the university library to get some materials. Joan asked to accompany him.

"Joan, I'd love to have you tag along. Are you sure you won't be bored while I look up things?"

"I'll bring something to read. I haven't finished the Agatha Christie book I checked out last week. I hope I can travel some day and see the places she describes in her books."

That settled she grabbed her novel and headed down the stairs to the car. Almost as soon as the car door was locked, Joan launched in.

"Dad, Janene told me that people, even colored people, like people better if they are light-skinned. I don't think that can be true. She said that you would already be a principal if you were lighter or a white man. That doesn't make sense. It can't be true, can it?"

"Joan, you're right and wrong in what you've just said. You can't judge a book by its cover and you can't tell the worth of a person by what's on the outside. There are others that believe that as well. For example, a young preacher named Martin Luther King, Jr. is trying to make just that point. You'd think he'd only have to preach that message to some whites, but unfortunately, Janene is correct as well."

"What do you mean? Is she right about you? Is that why Karen Smith didn't like me? What if the kids at Hyde Park don't like me? This is so unfair." The questions spilled out after having been pent up for so long.

"Hold on a minute. You've got to try to understand where all this came from. That doesn't make it right, but it helps if you know what you're up against." In a style and manner that Joan admired, her dad made history come alive as he took her back in time and brought her up to date.

"Though we could start this story well before slavery in America, we need a focal point, so let's begin there. You've learned in school that Africans were captured, brought to America, and sold mainly to white plantation owners in the South. Then a lot of history books jump to the Civil War and President Lincoln's Emancipation Proclamation which freed the slaves. Well, a great deal happened on the plantations between the start of slavery in America and its official end. Some of this isn't very pleasant. Do you want me to continue?

"Dad, you can't stop now," Joan implored.

"Well, for one thing, the Negro slaves were treated as chattel, that means property. They weren't thought of as real people. I personally think that the slave-owners had to think of their slaves as things because otherwise, how could they have treated them so inhumanely? Anyway, most of the original slaves were dark-skinned Africans who by the nature of their ordeal on the slave ships had to be very fit in order to have survived. These strong people were separated from their loved ones and sold to the highest bidder. Then they were taken to the plantations to work the fields, the cotton fields for the most part. Some of the slaves were trained to work in the master's house as cooks, butlers, and nannies, and the like. The slave master often took sexual liberties with the female slaves. These slave women gave birth to babies who, because they were half white, often had much lighter complexions than their mothers. These children, though still considered slaves, frequently received much better treatment than their darker brothers and sisters."

"Why did the slave women put up with this? What did they say? Couldn't they have pointed to the real fathers?"

"Remember, they weren't people; they were property. They had no rights. Because they and their children benefited from better treatment, they felt compelled to remain quiet. It was supposed to be a secret, but everyone was in on it. This led to a division among slaves. There were house-slaves and field-slaves. The house-slaves were better treated and they probably started to think of themselves as better. No one knew exactly what to do, so they basically tried to educate themselves, knowing that in time, this injustice would end. In the meantime, some escaped to the North and made new lives for themselves. Some, who could pass for white, left the whole situation behind; others fought and died to end the institution of slavery. Along the way, people learned that the lighter their skin, the better they were treated. Many started to see this as being the truth. They thought that because things were that way, things were supposed to be that way."

"But wasn't it the truth?" questioned Joan.

"Not really. It was what existed at the time. It wasn't right, so it wasn't the truth. Anyway, the Civil War came and divided the North and South. Slavery was one of the issues and the one that's important to your questions."

As Mr. Williams pulled the car into a parking space, Joan said, "That really explains it all."

"Not so fast, young lady," he responded after turning off the ignition and reaching for her hand. Looking down Joan saw his smooth, dark hand covering her own decidedly brown one. "That was a very brief overview, hitting only a few highlights. The whole story is much more involved and much more complex. I've tried to throw some light on your questions. I know you're an avid reader, but I never see you reading non-fiction for pleasure. Because your choices have been good, I haven't said anything. There are some books that might help you understand more about this problem. Things like the underground railroad, abolition, freedmen, and even the forming of the Territory of Colorado in 1861 are part of that historical fabric."

"You're right. This isn't simple. I think I have even more questions now. I just don't know what they all are."

"We can talk again whenever you want to, but let's get inside the library so I can get my materials. By being prepared and more qualified than the next man, I have been able to keep advancing. That's why this Ph.D. is so important to me. It's not just the extra pay that it'll mean. For me it's my key, my passport to wherever I want to go."

After shutting and locking the car door, they walked toward the library. Joan consciously left her Agatha Christie novel inside the car. She had decided instead to think about the many things her father had said. There was still so much to learn.

Chapter 5

Summer vacation came to an end and the first day of school was a reality. Beginnings always made Joan's stomach feel hollow. She wondered if she would ever outgrow this. Now she felt almost sick as she thought about the days ahead of her.

Hyde Park High School was everything she had dreamed it would be. She scored well above average on her reading and math tests and was placed in an accelerated learning program. She took biology her first year instead of general science; Latin was the foreign language she chose; advanced classes in history, English, and algebra, plus art and physical education rounded out her program.

A quick and capable student, Joan had no problem earning and maintaining an A average. She liked the hard work that was demanded of her. She liked the praise she received as a result of her efforts. All was going well, or so she thought.

One evening Joan was working a little later than usual on her algebra homework. She thought she had stumbled onto a shortcut for one type of problem and wanted to discuss it with her father, who was extremely good in math. Walking down the carpeted corridor to the living room, Joan was just about to enter when she was stopped by her father's voice.

"Where are all these friends that she's suppose to entertain? Where are the boys who wouldn't travel to the west side? In fact, where are the girl-friends she should be having over?"

"Dear, we haven't been here long enough. That's all. Just you wait. Before long you'll wish there weren't so many of her friends around," his wife said.

"Yes, Kitty, you're probably right. But we've been here almost five months. Betsy's had more people over than Joan. And it was for Joan's sake that we moved."

"Don't worry. Everything will be fine."

"I certainly hope you're right." But he didn't sound hopeful.

Joan realized she was eavesdropping and turned away. She tried to analyze what she had overheard. There was certainly no way she could forget what had been said. She forgot all about the algebra problem that a few moments ago had been so important.

Joan returned to her room and prepared for bed. All the time she was thinking about what she had just heard. It was true. She had not had many peo-ple over. Sometimes a classmate would stop by to do homework. But there had been no purely social visits. Joan tried to sleep, but sleep would not come. She was anxious about not living up to what was expected of her. She was worried about not pleasing both her parents.

Just before sleep overcame her, she decided to tackle the problem head-on. It was almost Christmas. She would give a party. Maybe she would even be invited to some.

When morning came it was an untroubled Joan who awoke. She had a plan and her doubts about its success passed with the early morning frost. A crisp, invigorating chill was in the air and Joan was ready for action.

The Christmas holiday season officially began the day after Thanksgiving. Joan's mother needed a new party dress because of the Lords and Ladies function to which she had been invited. Lords and Ladies was a young people's group that Betsy had been asked to join in September. Now they were having a Christmas party and the parents of members were included. Joan had not been asked to join.

Pretty little Betsy, with her long, light brown braids and sun-kissed complexion, had been filling her closet with party dresses since the move. Joan, however, had not needed a single dressy outfit. That had not bothered her until she overheard her parents' conversation.

Joan went with Betsy and her mother the Friday after Thanksgiving to shop for dresses. Even though Betsy already had a closet full of party wear, she, like her mother, wanted something different for the holiday. Caught up in the festive holiday spirit, Joan chose this time to make the first stage of her plan known.

"Mother, may I get a dress as well?"

"Oh, Joan, have you been invited to a party?" Before Joan could answer, her mother went on. "I think that's wonderful."

"Not yet, but I was thinking of asking if I could give a party."

"Of course you may." With that she embraced both daughters.

With that part settled, Joan went on to finally select an attractive red, wool dress that suited her very well. Her mother found a dress much more easily. Kitty Williams had a good figure and knew how to wear clothes. She looked like a model. Betsy also found a new outfit to her liking. She would look like a living doll in the Cinderella-type ball gown.

This time there was no need to disguise their purchases. Earlier in the summer, when they first moved to Hyde Park, her mother would use shopping bags from the pricier stores to hold purchases that were not really from those stores. This time, when they arrived at their bus stop in Hyde Park, the shopping bags read Bonwit Teller. All their dresses carried a Bonwit Teller label.

The remainder of the weekend was spent planning Joan's party. Giving events and clubs a French name was popular so Joan called her party

"*Soiree Chez Joan.*" Handwritten invitations were a must. In the lower corner of each was a discreet RSVP.

Joan mailed invitations to thirty of her classmates. The following week she waited for responses. As they came she made a careful list of all acceptances. By the Thursday before her party, twenty-three had said they would come, two had declined because of previous engagements, and the others had not answered at all. That surprised her a little because she saw each and every person on her list daily at school.

Saturday night came and a nervous Joan and her parents waited for the first guests. Joan had decided that "*huit heures et demie*" sounded grown-up so the party was scheduled from 8:30 until "*minuit.*" The Williamses did not really approve of youngsters being out so late, but Joan reasoned with them, saying this was a special evening for her and that the party would be chaperoned. She also added that since the guests were Hyde Parkers, they would not have far to travel.

Joan had toyed with the idea of asking two of her girlfriends from the old neighborhood to come. Eventually she rejected it. If she was to make a complete break with the west side, then it might not be prudent to mix the former friends with the new friends. Joan was hoping her decision was the right one as she, her parents, and Betsy listened for the sounds of cars arriving.

Joan was confident that all the party details had been attended to properly. Rather than peer anxiously from their semi-darkened living room window, as Betsy and her mother were doing, Joan decided a last check would not hurt. The dining room table, now moved against the wall, had its extra leaf installed and was covered with a green linen tablecloth. A large, lush, poinsettia plant in a white ceramic pot was the centerpiece. Holiday mints, jellied candies, as well as Spanish peanuts were in small crystal bowls that dotted the table in a random but artful pattern. The two bowls of punch, one red and the other green with the aid of food coloring, were to be brought in later. A friend from school who took printshop provided Joan with the hundred napkins she wanted. They were printed with an elegant, gold script that read *"Soiree Chez Joan."* Her mother did not know about these napkins. Now Joan placed them on the table. Next, the rheostat was turned to a low setting. Coupled with the lights from the Christmas tree in the living room, the party area took on a warm, inviting glow.

The doorbell rang. It was 8:50. Joan supposed it was Hyde Park chic to arrive late. To her 8:30 meant exactly that. Five guests were ushered in, four girls and a single boy. After being introduced to her parents and sister, the small group filed into the dining room. The Christmas music drifting in from the living room was replaced with fast dance music.

"That's a pretty red dress, Joan. I wish I could wear that color, but it clashes with my hair," said Elizabeth as she turned her perfectly coiffed red hair for all to admire.

Her brother, Gerald, also a redhead, reached out as if to touch his sister's hair. "Don't you dare," she hissed, stepping quickly out of his reach.

"Here are the records I said I'd bring," said Gerald as he handed Joan a stack.

"Thanks, and I'll take really good care of them. I'll return them tomorrow if that's OK."

"Well, I'm going to ..." but he never got to finish. The doorbell rang.

"Sorry, Gerald, but I've got to get that," and off she went.

This time the group consisted of three boys. Now the dancing could begin. More arrivals came and by ten, all but one expected guest was there.

Most people were dancing as often as they cared to. Someone had spiked the punch, but no one was getting out of hand. Just the same, Joan hoped her parents would not sample the punch. They would all get a real lecture if her father found out that the punch was spiked.

"I don't see an ashtray anywhere," a male voice said in a vexed tone.

"I guess that means no smoking," said another boy.

"Give me a break," said a displeased voice that Joan thought belonged to Elizabeth. Joan could not be sure because her back was turned to those talking. To turn around might seem too obvious.

Joan had not been asked to dance yet. She had been asked for more punch; she had been asked to change the music from fast to slow; she had been asked to refill the bowls of nuts and candies.

At 10:15 her mother summoned Joan to the door. "There's someone here to see you, but his name isn't on the guest list and he's not..."

Joan interrupted and said, "Oh, that must be Bernie," and went rapidly to the door.

"Bernie, I'm so glad you could make it. Let me take your coat," she said and handed it to her mother while simultaneously introducing the tall, skinny youth to her parents, Betsy having gone to her room after the first arrivals. Then to Bernie she said, "Come in where the food and dancing are."

"Sorry I'm late, but my shift at the restaurant just ended."

Bernie's slacks were just a bit too short, and the blue jacket did not exactly match his blue trousers. Thus it failed to give the effect of a suit that Bernie must have been trying for. His hands were large and calloused. But these observations were Joan's mother's, not Joan's. Bernie was not well-dressed. He seemed to have made an effort to look presentable, but Joan's mother rightly guessed he was not in the same league as the other male guests. It was this other group that Kitty wanted Joan to belong to. That was the purpose of the move.

Joan proudly escorted Bernie into the dining room and handed him some punch and nuts at once.

"These napkins are beautiful, Bernie. Are you sure I can't pay for them?"

"I'm sure, Joan. After all, the school supplied the ink and you gave me the napkins. I only set up the process and put the design on."

"Well, they are really lovely and I do appreciate..." This time it was Joan who did not get to finish.

It was Gerald. *A dance at last*, Joan thought. *And about time, too. It must be nearly 10:30.* Nevertheless, she did not mind the lateness of the request. Gerald was one of the most popular boys at school.

"Joan, excuse me, but I'd like to have my records. We're on our way to another party and I said I'd bring some records."

"Is it time for Nancy's party?" asked Jane.

"Almost. It starts at eleven and we'll have to be on time. She invites so many people that if you're late you might not get in," someone else added.

"Maybe we'll see you there, huh, Joan?" said Butch on his way out. "Everyone was invited."

Joan could think of at least one person who had not been invited. She was very tempted to lash out- but at whom? Butch was not the one responsible for Nancy's guest list. So instead of a cutting remark, she turned and went to the study to get the coats and her parents' assistance in handing them to her departing friends.

Chapter 6

Joan's mother knew that parents had brought some of Joan's friends. To Angela she said, "Isn't your father picking you up here in about an hour?"

"No, Mrs. Williams. I'm spending the night at Nancy's. After the boys leave, we have a slumber party. It's been this way for several years."

As the last guests were filing out, Joan's mother said to her daughter, "I know Nancy's mother. If you want me to call and suggest that your invitation got lost, I'm sure everything will work out."

"No. Don't do that. It wouldn't be right. Besides, my party isn't over yet." Joan directed her mother's attention to the lone figure standing by the dining room table, self-consciously selecting a candy from one crystal bowl and a few nuts from another.

"Bernie, are you staying awhile?" inquired Joan.

"Actually, I was just about to ask you for a dance when some of the records started to disappear." He said nothing of the people disappearing as well.

Kitty Williams chimed in at this point and said, "We have some smooth dancing music. My husband and I were just thinking about joining you kids for a dance when a slower tune was played."

Joan knew her mother was just trying to make conversation. The music had been slow tunes for most of the evening. She appreciated her mother's efforts to salvage the situation.

"We can certainly choose our own music now," added Joan's father as he placed some records on their turntable. Then he asked with mock gallantry as he embraced his wife, "Mrs. Williams, may I have the honor of this dance?" Before she had time to answer, he was guiding her gently around the floor to the soft, easy sounds of the Platters singing *Smoke Gets In Your Eyes*.

Taking his cue from Joan's father, Bernie said, "Miss Williams, may I have the pleasure of this dance?" He, however, waited for her reply.

"Yes, I can think of nothing I'd enjoy more." She, too, was caught up in the mood her father had projected.

After a few dances, Joan's parents retreated to the living room and finally to the study. At least once Joan's father ventured to the kitchen for a glass of water. At midnight Joan and Bernie concluded their last dance.

"Bernie, thanks for coming and the napkins were great." Then she added, though she had not really intended to bring it up, "Do you think you'll be too late for Nancy's?"

"I wasn't invited. I've never been invited to Nancy's. She only hangs around with real Hyde Parkers."

"But you *do* live in Hyde Park, Bernie," said Joan.

"Joan, you don't understand. It's not an address that I'm talking about. Some of that crowd comes from South Shore, Lake Meadows, Prairie Shores, and even the suburbs." He named affluent areas that were not geographically in Hyde Park. "Look, I've really got to go now. I'm working the early shift tomorrow. Trying to make all the cash I can this holiday." With that he squeezed her hand he was still holding, gave her a swift kiss on the cheek- just narrowly missing her lips, and was down the stairs.

When Joan closed her apartment door, she could hear the sound of her parents clearing up the dining room. Joan called into them, "I'm too tired to help now. Can I finish up in the morning?"

"There's not much to do. We'll be finished in no time at all. Sure, go to bed. By the way, these are very lovely napkins. Where did they come from?" asked Joan's mother.

"Oh, they're just one of the several surprises of the evening," she said as she walked down the hall to her bedroom.

Joan finally received her holiday party invitations. The ones she got were from girls who had attended her party. Joan accepted the first invitation gladly and anticipated an enjoyable evening full of laughing and dancing. Based on her earlier conversation with Bernie, she knew he would not be at Mary Beth's party. That had not dampened her enthusiasm for long. Joan realized that Bernie rarely went out socially because of his studies, his job, and his sports activities. *Besides*, thought Joan, *I am a real Hyde Parker. Betsy belongs to Lords and Ladies, Mother joined the local ladies bridge groups, and Dad is on two community boards.*

Joan needed party dresses so she and her mother made another trip downtown. This time they made a real day of it. After purchasing an emerald green velveteen dress at Field's, they had lunch in the store's Tea Room. A fashion show was in progress. As they watched the models and ate club sandwiches and drank Cokes, the two of them talked about parties and boys.

"Joan, I think it would be perfectly acceptable to take an escort with you," her mother said, picking up the thread of a previous discussion.

"But Mother, when the invitation was extended, it was to me only. It said nothing about an escort. These kids take guest lists seriously. I wouldn't want to embarrass anyone."

"I suppose you may be right. When I was growing up it was understood that a single girl could bring an escort. But you know your group better than I do," said Joan's mother just before putting an olive in her mouth.

"And I'll know most of the kids from school. I won't have any problems finding people to be with." Joan did not add how difficult it was to try to be with this group at school. She was still an outsider.

With that apparently settled, they turned their attention fully to the fashion show. Thin, young women wearing resort clothing did not appeal to Joan. It was cold in Chicago and summer was a long way off. Kitty, however, was fascinated by the fashions and at one point said to Joan, "If your father and I could take a winter vacation, I'd love to have that orange outfit. It's so tropical and just a little daring."

After lunch they looked at more dresses, but they could only decide on one of them. Their day's shopping completed, they rode back to Hyde Park. Joan immediately opened the box containing the green dress and steamed out the few wrinkles in the bathroom as she showered. She then pin curled her short, dark hair and settled down to read *Rebecca* until time to get ready for Mary Beth's party. The story absorbed her at once. Thus it was with reluctance that she put the novel aside just prior to Rebecca's entrance at her own ball.

Mary Beth's party was scheduled to begin at nine. Joan decided that being exactly on time was not necessary. She was on the guest list so she felt a punctual arrival was not mandatory. Tonight it was important that she look her best. Using a

Seventeen Magazine as a guide, she began carefully copying a model's make-up.

Every little detail was attended to with equal care- from the pale pink lipstick to the soft green eyeshadow. Using a model's trick she had read about, she put a scarf over her head and then slipped into the emerald gown. Removing the scarf, she placed it around her shoulders and began to unpin her hair. She brushed and combed, and shaped and reshaped until every strand was in place. A wisp of hairspray and touch of Miss Dior cologne completed her preparations.

"You look simply stunning tonight," her father said when he saw his older daughter. And he meant it.

"Thanks, Dad," Joan said as she took her gray Sunday coat from the front closet.

The ride to Mary Beth's house only took a few minutes. Shortly, Joan found herself in front of the house. It was 9:15. It was also the first time Joan had ever been late for anything. She savored the good feeling this gave her and breathed in the cold, night air.

"I'll pick you up at midnight," Joan's father called after her as she walked to Mary Beth's door.

Joan rang the bell and introduced herself to the woman inside. Joan's name was confirmed against the guest list and then her coat was asked for. After that she was directed to the recreation room where the party seemed in full swing.

There was a brief moment when everyone stopped to look toward the newcomer. To Joan it seemed like an eternity. All eyes were upon her. She had the undivided attention of all the party-goers.

Now everyone will know I'm a real Hyde Parker, she thought. In that moment of almost total silence, there was only one voice that was heard.

"That's what I thought she'd look like," some girl said. There was derision in the tone.

Joan spent the rest of the evening trying to pretend that she had not heard that cutting remark. Mentally she constructed numerous possibilities concerning what she heard. However, they all came back to the seven hurtful words.

During the evening, a few people spoke to her. Several boys asked her to dance, but each only asked for one dance. Nobody commented on how nice she looked. Everyone who did speak thanked her for her lovely party. Well before midnight, Joan knew the reason for this invitation. It was a payback- en masse. Suddenly she remembered the first week of school when she sat down for lunch with what looked like a friendly group of kids. They were talking and laughing comfortably until she sat down. They all seemed to remember that they had to be elsewhere and left her to her solitary lunch. The hollow feeling in the pit of her stomach she felt then recurred. Fighting back tears, she managed to get through the rest of the evening.

When she got into her father's car around midnight, she said before being asked, "It was a lovely party." In her mind, the words running through it were *pay back, pay back, pay back,* and *hurtful, small-minded people.*

Chapter 1

There were two other invitations. These Joan politely refused. Kitty was upset about the refusal and asked, "But, Joan, why don't you want to go?"

"Mother, there's a lot of reading I have to do just to keep up with the kids at Hyde Park," Joan lied. She knew that using academics as an excuse would work with her mother.

"In that case, you're absolutely right," said a mollified Kitty.

Joan did not enjoy lying to her mother and it surprised her that the lie came so easily. Joan had not read as extensively as some of her classmates, that at least was true. She was near the top of her class nevertheless. Suddenly she was not content with being near the top. She wanted to be the top student. Joan wanted to show everyone that she was just as good and maybe even better than they were.

Reading and studying came easily for Joan. Instead of the many friends her classmates shared, she came to know and understand the characters who populated the novels and plays she read.

Hardy, Dickens, Austen, Bronte, and Shakespeare became her companions. As she began reading non-fiction more intensely, the complex histories of nations, old as well as new, fascinated her. As her father had suggested, she began reading about race issues and civil rights in America. She knew she had a great deal of lost time to make up for in those areas. Algebraic equations became for her what crossword puzzles were for other people. Science and Latin absorbed her totally. So at the end of her first year of high school Joan had a straight A average and was asked to join the National Honor Society for the coming year. She was one of the three straight A students in the freshman class, but the only girl to achieve that distinction, and the sole minority student.

Joan knew her mother would want her to take a break from her studies for the summer. Joan had other plans. With Bernie's help, she knew she could succeed.

Bernie had a cousin who attended the University of Chicago on a partial scholarship. She had just completed her first year. Louise lived with Bernie's family as a way of saving money so she could afford the rest of the tuition. She worked at the school's library as well. Joan had Bernie introduce her to Louise. Both girls hit it off at once.

Joan explained to Louise what her first year at Hyde Park had been like. She told her how she had taken refuge in her studies. She told her that the color barrier was hard to break down. So, as her father was doing, Joan looked to education. There was still competition to face and Joan wanted to stay on top.

"So you see my problem," Joan concluded after the long explanation.

"Yes, I certainly do," said Louise. "It's much the same with me except that I have to maintain a B average to keep my scholarship. Bernie doesn't face the same problem right now, even though he's dark. He plays great basketball and the team needs someone of his caliber. Too bad he's not recognized for his intellect. He's quite intelligent. It runs in our family," Louise added with a smile. "Of course I'll help you with your plan."

With that, they put the finishing touches on their arrangement. Louise would permit Joan to use the library facilities any evening she was on duty. If Joan needed to check out materials, Louise would do so on her own card. In return, all Joan had to do was to keep their agreement a secret and never keep a book past its due date.

Thus began Joan's summer campaign. During the day she took Betsy to her various meetings, lessons, or to her friends' homes. Betsy was learning to play the piano, but it was Joan who found the symbols of piano music intriguing. Her curiosity was aroused; there was nothing she could do but decipher the notes. She began to teach herself to play and before long, she was more accomplished than Betsy, who was an indifferent player and would probably remain one.

Several evenings during the week, Bernie would call for Joan. Sometimes he would ask her to go to a movie, sometimes to go for a soda at the nearby drugstore; at other times, he would ask her just to go for a walk. Joan always accepted. Kitty was not particularly pleased with Joan's choice of a male companion. He was not the type of Hyde Park boy she wanted her daughter to date; but she said very little about it to Joan and was always polite to Bernie.

Each date followed a pre-established pattern. Bernie would come by for Joan and walk her to the library. He would then continue to his job. After work he would pick her up from the library and take her home. One evening things were different.

"Joan, I've got a night off and would really like to take you out. Would you like to go downtown to the State and Lake to see a movie?"

"That sounds great!" She was genuinely happy. It was the first time a boy had ever asked her out. Almost at once she began to have misgivings. *What would happen*, she wondered, *if the date wasn't successful? What would happen to the summer as planned?* She did not want to endanger her carefully laid summer scheme. She was making such progress. It was only the end of July. Although she had almost completed the readings for her sophomore English class, there was more to do.

Joan's next year's teacher had been only too happy to intimidate the soon-to-be sophomore honor's English class with the names of authors and titles of selections they would encounter. While everyone was busy groaning under the anticipated weight of the assignments, Joan was writing furiously. She did not want to miss a single title or name. During her summer library time, she not only read the selections, but she also took notes on what the critics said of these notables. As soon as her English readings were completed, she would tackle the history course, reading and taking notes and perhaps even delving into supplemental topics. Geometry, for which she had a natural bent, science, and Latin would come last. She was already the best first-year Latin student. With all that was at stake, she did not want a failed romance to get in her way.

On the other hand, she could not let Bernie think that she was simply using him. Mentally she tripped over those words. *I'm not using him*, she thought. *I really like him as a friend. He's easy to be with and he doesn't make demands.*

Therefore, in answer to his request, Joan said, "I'd be delighted to go to the movies with you."

"Great. Maybe we can have a soda afterwards and talk about the picture. You're the kind of girl a guy can talk to."

So that was it. She was the kind of girl a boy could talk to. That had been what she was after.

She wanted people to know her for her intellect. Her plan was working all too well.

Joan did not have to invent a story for this date. She merely told her parents the truth. "Bernie wants to take me downtown for a movie this Friday," she announced rather than asked at the dinner table the evening following the call.

"Don't you think you're seeing too much of him?" asked Kitty, unable to keep her feelings concealed any longer.

Joan's first impulse was to tell her parents exactly what had been going on between them. Then she felt she might hurt them by revealing her harmless deception. So instead she commented, "We haven't been downtown for a show. This is really something quite special."

"Joanie likes Bernie. Joanie likes Bernie." sing-songed Betsy.

Joan glared at Betsy, but before she could say anything to her sister, her father said, "That's enough, Betsy."

Betsy's song may have been abruptly ended, but she had more to say. "Well, it must be true. They spend so much time together."

"But is it alright if I go?" said Joan, ignoring Betsy and returning to her dutiful daughter role.

Joan's father looked at his wife before answering. Then he said, "You must be home by eleven, and you should take some change with you in case you need to call home."

Joan smiled in appreciation. Inwardly she was thinking that all Bernie had on his mind was discussing the movie. That would have been a relief to her father.

Friday night came and Joan found herself taking more time than usual with her appearance. Again she referred to one of the ingenues in *Seventeen Magazine* and painted her face exactly like the one she chose. Joan had not yet mastered the technique of applying make-up. The other girls she knew actually looked as though they had just stepped out of a magazine picture. Their fair or very light complexions looked freshly scrubbed with hints of pink around their cheeks and soft pastels around their light eyes. Their golden brown hair caught the sun. Joan, with her swarthy coloring, found it a hard task to make herself look like them without appearing as though she were dressed for a circus. Her dark, short hair gleamed, and she was certain the 100 brush strokes she religiously gave her hair every night were responsible. Finishing with a touch of pink lipstick, and dabbing Miss Dior on all of her pulse points, she was ready- ready to talk and to be talked to.

Chapter 8

Bernie arrived promptly at 6:30 for Joan. He had borrowed his brother's convertible, which was old but gleaming. The top was down and the slight breeze felt good. It was a welcome relief from the sweltering Chicago heat. Bernie headed east on Hyde Park Boulevard and then connected with the Outer Drive. Cautiously he merged with the oncoming traffic and went north towards the Loop, as the downtown area was known. At this new speed, the gentle breeze turned into a real wind. By the time they reached the parking lot, not a hair on Joan's head was in place and her freshly scrubbed face felt dirty and gritty.

Sensing her discomfort and realizing the cause of it, Bernie apologetically said, "Gee, Joan, I didn't think about putting the top up."

"That's alright, Bernie. I can repair the damage in the restroom. Just give me a couple of minutes before we take our seats."

Joan did what she could in the ladies room of the State and Lake Theater. It was not just the grime she wiped away as she saw herself in the elegant, gilt-edged mirror. A few tears needed taking care of also.

Joan pulled herself together and rejoined her companion, who had in the meantime purchased them two large boxes of buttered popcorn. Handing one box to Joan, he said, "It's not a dozen long-stemmed roses, but it's for the nicest girl I know."

"Thanks, Bernie. You're so thoughtful. I always feel I owe you lots of thank yous for so many things like —" But she trailed off rather than complete the thought she had begun.

"Don't worry. You'll come through. Let's get our seats while there's still some choice left. And Joan, you look very pretty tonight and —" He, too, trailed off without finishing his thought.

They entered the darkened movie theater as previews of coming attractions were flashing across the screen. Finding seats to their liking, they settled into the plush, velvet cushions and prepared to enjoy the feature.

Occasionally during the movie, Bernie's right hand, which he had wrapped around her seat, brushed her shoulder. That was alright, but she wondered what to do if his hand should move to less neutral parts of her body. She was sure some definite reaction would be called for. But Bernie's hand did not roam. He was a perfect gentleman. Her parents had told her to act like a lady if she wanted to be treated as a lady. Apparently they were correct.

After the movie Bernie suggested going to a nearby Walgreen's Drugstore for a soda or sundae. Joan checked her watch to verify the time. She knew better that to break her 11:00 curfew.

"I'd like that, Bernie, but I must be home by eleven."

"OK, Cinderella, we'll eat and talk and I promise you'll be home on time. After all, I've never made you late yet," he chuckled.

They walked to the drugstore, took a booth, and ordered their sundaes. Joan asked for a cherry one while Bernie had pineapple. Sitting with their picture-perfect ice cream they began to discuss the movie.

"Well, Joan. Explain it to me. *Last Year at Marienbad* was too deep for me."

"Bernie, I hate to tell you this, but one viewing wasn't enough for me either. I liked what I saw, but I'm not sure what I saw, if you know what I mean."

"At least your admission reassures me. I suppose I'm not just a dumb jock."

"Who said you were?" inquired Joan with genuine concern.

"Nobody in particular and everybody in general," he said seriously.

"Well 'nobody' and 'everybody' are mistaken. You're intelligent and sincere and —" she hesitated.

"And what, Joan?" he prompted.

"And a great friend."

"Is it possible that we can be more than friends? I'd like you to be my special girl."

"You've asked me two very difficult questions tonight- one about a movie and one about my life. And I don't have an answer for either yet."

"You don't have to answer me right now. Think about it."

"Can we remain friends even if I'm not your special girl?"

"Now you just asked me a very difficult question and I don't have an answer."

After that last remark Bernie picked up their bill, left a generous tip, and paid the cashier. They walked to the parking lot to collect the car. Bernie had raised the convertible's top before leaving it in the lot, so the top was up when an attendant delivered the car.

"You want me to leave the top up for the drive back?" Bernie asked.

"Yes. No, let it down. I think I'll enjoy the air this time."

The ride back to Hyde Park was made mostly in silence. Bernie had turned on the radio and they listened to Herb Kent, the Cool Gent, talk about this record and that. Joan and Bernie said very little to one another. They actually had a great deal to say but elected to say nothing.

About twenty minutes after leaving the parking lot, Bernie pulled his brother's car in front of Joan's house. Ever the gentleman, he got out of the car, crossed over to her side, and opened the door for her. He then escorted her through the perfectly appointed and maintained vestibule, and up the stairs to her apartment.

"Thanks for a lovely evening," said Joan as she tentatively offered her right hand to Bernie.

Taking the tips of her fingers and touching them to his lips, he said, "Thank you, Joan. I really enjoyed tonight, even though we didn't talk about the movie."

Suddenly he released her hand, cupped her face in his hands, and kissed her full on the lips. Just as suddenly he bounded down the stairs and was out of the front door.

Chapter 9

Joan noticed the light in the study as she walked down the now carpeted hallway to her room. Her father had taken and passed the principal's examination and had recently been given the top assignment at another west side school. He had more work to do before his doctoral dissertation would be ready. That new degree would bring in additional income. Joan remembered her father telling her why doing extremely well academically was a strong point with him. No one had ever scored higher on the principal's exam and no other principal candidate was currently near completion of a Ph.D. at the prestigious University of Chicago. The extra money that accompanied his current promotion was being spent now, making their home as attractive and comfortable as possible. Expecting to bid both her parents good night, Joan quietly entered the study.

Her father was deeply engrossed in his writing and did not notice her entrance. Joan cleared her throat and said, "If you're busy, Dad, I'll just say good night. But I thought you'd want to know that I made my curfew. Where's Mother?"

"She's playing bridge with some friends, I don't expect her until around midnight. Did you enjoy the movie?"

"It was a bit hard to understand from just watching it once. I bet you would have liked it. But it's not the movie I want to talk about."

"Come and sit down. I could use a break," said her father as he got up from his desk and walked over to the sofa where Joan was sitting.

"Remember how we always talked when I rode around with you when we lived on the west side?"

"Of course, I do. I sure miss those talks. We haven't had a really long one since, let me see. I think it was the summer before your freshman year at Hyde Park. I guess you and Bernie talk now."

"Not really, but Bernie's who I want to talk about. First I have a small confession to make. All those evenings he's been taking me out- well, he's been dropping me off at the U of C library and picking me up on his way home from work."

Joan told her father all about her summer plan and then came to the crucial point. "Now Bernie's asked me to go with him, that is, to be his —"

"I understand the idiom," her father interrupted. When Joan did not continue, he said, "Go on, Joan. Don't stop at this point in your story."

"There isn't any more to tell. I just don't know what to do."

"I know you better than to presume that you want me to make a decision for you. Instead I'll be your mentor." A moment later he continued, "Do you like Bernie well enough to be his girl?"

"I don't know."

"How will your relationship with him be affected if you turn him down?"

"I asked him about that. He didn't know."

"Do you want to go with any boy at this time?"

"I don't know," was again the response. After a short pause she said, "Dad, you're wonderful. I knew you'd help me see what should have been clear to me all along."

"I'm glad I helped although I'm not exactly sure that I should take so much of the credit. I can tell you this, though. I'm relieved knowing about the library. I saw you there one night when I was picking up a book. I thought perhaps you and Bernie had an argument. I also wondered how you got in."

"Oh, Dad, I'm so happy everything's out in the open — at least between us."

Joan got up from the sofa and left the study. Tonight she was too tired to read before going to sleep. Instead of reading one more chapter of *The Man in the Iron Mask*, she prepared for bed and went immediately to sleep.

Sunday was already hot and sticky when Joan awakened. But her spirits were high because of her heart-to-heart talk with her father. When she entered the kitchen, her mother and Betsy were in a deep discussion about a party dress.

"But, Mommie, I can't wear that dress again. Everyone's seen it a hundred times."

"Betsy," said her mother patiently but persistently, "you can not have a new dress for every party you —"

"I don't want a new dress for every party, just for this one."

"Betsy, you may not have a new dress, but," her mother raised her hand to silence Betsy before she could interrupt again, "we can have one changed or dyed so it doesn't look the same."

"If I can't have a new dress I guess changing one'll be alright." Brightening a bit, Betsy asked, "Could my white one be dyed a pale lilac? I don't have a dress that color."

"Yes, I think that would suit you. It's nice to able to wear so many shades well. You and I are quite fortunate to have —" Kitty swallowed the words that she was about to utter. Joan had heard that phrase or similar ones so often that not saying it had no effect. Joan was not going to let anything dampen her spirits. After all, she had her life's course to plot.

Bernie called that afternoon to ask Joan if she had thought about going with him. "Bernie, I'm flattered that you asked me. I really am. But I'm just not ready to go steady." In her mind Joan could hear the remarks that would surely be made if she and Bernie became a pair: *Joan and the*

Jock, or *she couldn't get anyone else*, or worse yet, *he could have done better*.

"I'm sorry that's your decision. But I can't say it comes as a surprise."

"What do you mean, it's no surprise? I didn't know the answer myself until a little while ago," said Joan, annoyed at being second-guessed.

"I mean you're looking for some Prince Charming, some preconceived, non-existent person."

"No, I'm not. I'm not looking for anyone, least of all you." Those last words just slipped out and once out could not be taken back. *It serves him right*, she thought. *Who is he to put me on the spot like that?*

"Good-bye, Joan. Don't think it hasn't been nice." Then the line went dead.

Joan went to the library that evening and talked with Bernie's cousin, Louise. "I guess you know what happened," Joan began.

"Yes, but I'm glad you didn't lead him on."

"You are? I thought you'd be mad at me. Blood is thicker than water and all of that."

"That's great as a cliche, but life isn't always like that. I admire what you're trying to accomplish and I admire you for being honest with Bernie. So enough said. You'd better get busy. The library isn't open all night."

The two girls understood one another. There was nothing else to say. So Joan's summer plan continued according to schedule. Now her father picked her up when she finished in the evenings instead of Bernie.

As a result, Joan's sophomore year went according to plan. She earned a straight A average the first marking period and by the end of the first semester, her name was known around the school. She had established herself as the number one student in her class and one of the most able students in the history of the school. Academically things had gone extremely well. There was little to report on the social scene. If people could not accept her brown skin, they certainly could not deny her intelligence. She still wanted to be accepted socially. She would continue to work on that.

Chapter 10

Joan did not need to employ a plan to get ahead for her junior year. She would have to figure out how to get around her mother's usual attempts to get her involved with some Hyde Park boy. Kitty Williams had been relieved when Joan and Bernie broke up. She had never been told the real story. She really did not know why Joan was having such trouble making friends. And Kitty was more than happy to have a bright daughter whose talents were recognized. She also wanted her daughter to date- to date the right young man.

Joan would turn sixteen over the summer. "Sweet sixteen and never been kissed." That was very nearly the truth. Toying with the idea of becoming sixteen gave Joan just the idea she was searching for. Now she would merely wait until the opportunity came to put her plan into motion.

That opportunity came one Saturday morning in June, shortly before school ended for the year. Betsy had been invited to spend some time with the Baker family in Union Pier, Michigan. Many of Kitty's new friends had cabins there which they used periodically throughout the summer months. These were not summer homes, just comfortable places where one could spend time on the beach and away from the city. It was this invitation that Betsy and her mother were discussing when Joan came in for breakfast.

"It's a lovely idea, but I think you had better accept for a definite period," said Kitty.

"Oh, Mommie! Why can't I stay for as long as they'll let me?"

"Because that would be imposing, taking advantage of their offer and —"

"But they wouldn't have asked me it they didn't want me to come," interrupted Betsy.

"Betsy," said her father sternly, "you must learn not to speak while someone else is still talking. It's an unpleasant habit in an otherwise pleasant young lady."

Put in her place and flattered as well, Betsy said, "I'm sorry, Mommie. What were you going to say?"

"Well, I've lost the exact words I had in mind, but the point was this. You should accept for two weeks. Besides, you don't want to take too much sun. I can still recall the time you went to camp before we moved here. When I came to pick you up, you were so dark I didn't recognize you immediately. Do you remember?"

"No, I don't remember that. I don't remember much about where we used to live. It seems so long ago. But you don't have to worry. Melissa and Tiffany won't want to get much sun. They like being light."

"Well, you're settled for the summer. And of course there'll be the normal Lords and Ladies activities. But what will we do with you, Joan?" Kitty said as she turned her attention to her older daughter.

The time was here and Joan handled her lines superbly. "Mother, I'll be sixteen in August. I want to have a Sweet Sixteen Party. I want it to be better than the Christmas party I gave."

"Oh, Joan, what a wonderful idea. There'll be so much to do- caterers, invitations, guest list, and of course, your dress. There'll hardly be time for anything else. A well-planned party takes a great deal of effort."

"Yes, Mother, I think you're right. We'll have to focus all our attention on the party." Joan was not sure, but she thought her father winked at her.

Breakfast ended on a happy note. Everyone had something to do for the summer. Joan's parents even managed to include a week's vacation for themselves on Paradise Island in the Bahamas. Joan and Betsy would be cared for by the family who lived on the first floor of their building, a childless, middle-aged couple the Williamses had befriended.

It would be almost the end of July when the Williamses returned so much of the planning for the birthday party had to be done before the

Bahamas trip. Kitty planned to call one of her Hyde Park friends to get the name of a reliable catering service. But Joan was adamant about not contacting anyone they may have offered. Instead she suggested they use the Yellow Pages of the telephone directory. By relying on the size of the ad and the length of time the business had been in operation, Joan was confident that a reputable company could be found. Using that method, they discovered one to their liking and made an appointment to discuss selections and other necessary arrangements.

Joan recalled that for her Christmas party, the fare had been simple. This time there was no hesitancy on either parent's part about engaging a caterer. This bothered Joan a little. She was not sure how they had the money for an elaborate party and a vacation out of the country as well. Finally Joan's curiosity got the better of her and she asked her mother about their finances.

Kitty Williams laughed when she heard the question, but went on to put Joan's mind at ease. "Sweetheart," she said, "except for the necessities of life and a few gifts here and there, I've hardly had to spend a thing on you. The last really big items were those dresses for the parties our first Christmas in Hyde Park. It's a pleasure to be able to do something like this for you. You require so little."

Materially Joan knew that what her mother said was accurate. There were other things that Joan required.   Being accepted for what she is was at the top of her list. Money could not buy that.

A birthday dress had to be purchased and Kitty made a production of it as she did with most things. This time Kitty suggested that they look at Saks Fifth Avenue as well as some of the boutiques on North Michigan Avenue before making a decision.   This meant a couple of trips to the Magnificent Mile, as this shopping area was known, and a couple of lunches as well. Shopping without stopping for lunch was not shopping to Joan's mother. This also meant additional opportunities for Kitty to talk to Joan about boys.

But Joan wanted to avoid that subject. She did not have enough to say to hold a decent conversation. She liked boys well enough, but seemingly the feeling was not reciprocated. End of conversation. It was too hurtful for her to tell her mother the real reason. Joan knew her mother could not possibly understand.

There was, however, something that Joan wanted to discuss. She wanted to know why, after all these years, her mother and father had been invited to visit her grandparents. The DuPuis had never come to Chicago to see them. Very few phone calls were exchanged and gifts rarely arrived from them. Neither could Joan remember her family visiting them in New Orleans. To her, her grandparents were the two people in the picture frame on her mother's nightstand.

Over their break for lunch during their firs
dress-finding trip, Joan inquired about the impend-
ing trip to New Orleans. "When was the last time
you saw your parents? It must have been a long
time ago."

"Joan, it wasn't until recently that we were
invited," was the candid answer.

"But why do you need an invitation to see you
own parents? Can't you just go there anytime you
want to?"

"I could go at any time, but what I said was
that, we had not been asked until recently. The
invitations never included your father, or even you,
for that matter. Those were some hard times after
I married your father. It's only been since we've
moved to Hyde Park that I even let them know
about Betsy. But now you might say that the cold
war between the DuPuis and the Williamses is
thawing."

"But why are you at- -at war?"

"It's a long story, but it's one you ought to
know."

Eating, but not tasting the Chinese food before
her, Joan listened spellbound as her mother
unfolded a tale that would mark the end of Joan's
innocence.

Chapter 11

"I was born Antoinette Catherine DuPuis, the only daughter of a prosperous, long-established Creole family in New Orleans. I grew up in a sheltered environment and at the top of a rigid and complex caste system. But of course, I didn't know that then. I was five before Mother allowed me to speak English inside of our home. French was the language of some of her ancestors, and French was the language that she insisted be used at home. And she always called me by my given name, 'Antoinette Catherine.' When I entered school, my classmates found that quite a mouthful, so they began to call me Kitty and it stuck. Although Mother never permitted herself to use my nickname, Father called me Kitty whenever she wasn't around.

"I had a brother who was eight years my senior. Robert Jean DuPuis was the splitting image of my father- tall, fair, blond, and blue-eyed. My parents were always quick to say that they had one white child and one almost-white child. That counted for a great deal in their closed society.

"Everyone, my parents included, would tell me what a beautiful child I was. But I couldn't see why I was singled out. I used to have waist-length hair then, but there were other girls with long hair. In fact, I thought most of us looked remarkably alike— chiseled features, light hair and light eyes. But somehow the adults felt that my particular combination of olive complexion, hazel eyes, and golden brown hair was special. I used to think that some of the girls who were as fair and blond as Robert Jean were the prettiest."

"Mother, I didn't know that you had a brother," interrupted Joan. "Where is Uncle Robert Jean now?"

Kitty laughed, but there was a shallowness in it. Then she answered, "Robert Jean went off to the army and walked totally into the other world. Every once in awhile a postcard would arrive from an exotic place. But there was never a return address."

"Oh, how sad. I know your parents were upset by that."

"Strangely enough they weren't. I think they just missed not knowing how well he was making out in the other world." Then Kitty returned to her own story. "Life was idyllic for me. There were parties, really nice ones in very large homes. We gave some of the best parties and had one of the largest homes. There were ballet lessons and piano lessons. There were voice lessons and cooking lessons. And of course, there were the sessions with my French tutor. With all those activities I was only an average student in school. I did take the right classes for college entrance and because of my fluency in French, I was able to place out of the first two years of college French.

"I left Louisiana only once and that was to travel to Washington, D.C., to attend Howard University. I'm sure it was the letters of recommendation and my placement test scores, more than my grades, that were responsible for my admittance. I became a serious student because I knew I'd be asked to leave Howard if I didn't get decent grades. The first year was rough because I didn't have good study habits. Fortunately French was easy, even at the junior level, and that left me more time to prepare for my other subjects. I ended my freshman year with a hard-earned B minus average. My sophomore year was a bit easier because I had the knack of studying. I majored in elementary education and minored in French literature. That's how I met your father."

At the mention of her father, Joan leaned a little closer. She did not want to miss anything her mother had to say, especially about her dad.

"Clarence was studying French literature as a second minor. He was a graduate student in counseling and guidance with a mathematics and French minor. He never did believe in doing things the easy way. We met when I was in the library inquiring about a French book. He liked my accent, he told me later. I liked him at once.

"Clarence was tall, dark, and if not handsome, striking. He had a presence. When he walked into a room, you could feel he was there even before you saw him. It's still like that. I know when he's near. Anyway, we began dating seriously almost at once. He would complete his master's degree that June and would begin working at Dunbar in D.C. Before school ended for the summer, he had asked me to marry him. I eagerly accepted and only had to figure out how to introduce him to my parents.

"I went home to New Orleans for the summer and told my parents that I was engaged to the fellow I'd been writing them about. They were elated. They wanted to meet him. Since we weren't going to marry until I had graduated, we decided that they would meet him during the Christmas holidays when they would come to Washington for a visit. When they returned to New Orleans, they could formally announce my engagement. That met with Clarence's approval, and he said we would wait until December to select my engagement ring."

Chapter 12

"School resumed in the fall and I threw myself into my studies. This was my senior year and I was determined to excel. Some special weekends Clarence and I would go to a play, or out to dinner, or to an opera. Most often we'd just go to a museum because he was saving money for our future. I could hardly wait for the Christmas holidays because I would see more of him.

"At last the vacation period began and my parents arrived and took a suite at the Hilton. They asked me to join them. No sense in my staying in the dorm while they were here. I packed my nicest clothes and moved in with them. It was great. Just like being at home. My second night with them was the night that Clarence invited them out to dinner. He chose Gadsby's in Old Town Alexandria because the food and service were good and because it had atmosphere.

"We each, my mother, father, and I, prepared for this dinner with special care. We took a cab to Gadsby's. Our table was ready when we arrived at seven forty-five. There was a message for me that

Clarence would be there by eight and to go ahead and order cocktails for everyone. My mother was impressed by his thoughtfulness and said, 'What a nice young man he must be.' While sipping her cocktail, she kept an eye on the door, noting each new arrival. When a tall, blond man of about twenty-five entered, she said, 'Oh, that must be Clarence.' I loved to hear her pronounce his name. She said it as only the French can. But I didn't have to look up. I knew it wasn't he. A few minutes later another tall, blond approached our table, nodded to my father and bid me a Merry Christmas. He was a fellow I knew and after giving his greeting, he continued on to his table. Mother sighed as he walked on.

"At precisely eight o'clock, Clarence entered. I didn't have to look up to know that he was there. He was immaculately attired and caused quite a few heads to turn. It was with great pride that I introduced him to my parents. Sitting with me that evening were all the people I loved best in the world.

"My parents were formal and cold in their responses. Small talk was made, but the real purpose of this dinner was not brought up by them. Clarence immediately caught the iciness of my parents' greeting. It was in such sharp contrast to my own. He told me later that he had encountered thinly veiled hostility before but never from people who were so important to him. He realized that he couldn't change attitudes overnight, so he tried to relax and be himself. I was so embarrassed by my parents' actions that I was fighting off tears for most of the dinner.

"But Clarence came to my rescue by seeming not to notice my parents' rudeness. I remember that conversation as though it took place yesterday. 'Kitty and I are so happy that you could join us for dinner on this momentous occasion,' he'd said. In the meantime he had pulled his seat nearer to what could pass as the head of the table. He just took complete charge and any attempt to guide the conversation away from its true purpose was met with polite resistance.

"During the middle of dessert, Clarence asked my father for my hand in marriage. Dad had a mouthful of food and had to wait a few seconds before responding. Those few seconds were costly for him. Any advantage he had hoped to gain was irretrievably lost. 'Mr. Williams,' he began.

"But Clarence cut in and said, 'Call me Clarence, please.' It was more of a command than a request.

"So my father tried again. 'Clarence, it isn't every day that a father gets asked such an important question.'

"'It isn't every day, sir, that a man asks such an important question. I am very much in love with your daughter and she loves me. I have a good job, a promising future, and money in the bank. She hasn't met my parents yet, but I'm sure they'll like her.'

"He winked at me and added, 'I'm confident they'll accept my choice although my mother can be very critical.'

"Then my mother got into the act and tried to help out father. She said, 'Antoinette Catherine, don't you think you should think this over some more? Marriage is a very big step.'

"But I was having nothing to do with Mother trying to treat me like a child. And so I said to her, 'I have thought about this and little else since Clarence first asked me to marry him. And now I am not simply thinking about getting married, I am planning to get married.' Somehow we finished the meal without calling too much attention to ourselves. Clarence told my father that we would be selecting my ring and discussing wedding plans.

"The rest of the holiday was spent looking for a ring and deciding on other things we'd need. Life at the hotel wasn't much fun anymore so I spent as much time away from my parents as possible. Clarence and I selected a fiery solitaire from J.E. Caldwell Company, picked a wedding date and place and decided not to risk another dinner to announce our decisions.

"We chose the last night of my folks' visit to give them the rest of the news. Clarence came by the Hilton to wish my parents a safe trip home. Then he and I went to a play. He promised to have me back early, as he figured we'd have lots to talk about before they left. Clarence then told them that we would be getting married a year from now in Martinique. I would meet his parents this spring in Martinique and he assured my mother and father that I would be well chaperoned. I took the opportunity to tell my parents that his family was a prominent one and would do nothing to bring dishonor on themselves. I even added that I hoped they accepted me. That sent my folks reeling. 'Not accept you!' they said in unison. 'Yes, not accept me. They may have had other plans for their son.'"

Chapter 13

Kitty paused to sip some of the now cold tea from her cup and then brought the narrative to its conclusion. "I went to Martinique in the spring and met the Williams family. They were warm, friendly people, and I took to them right away. They hugged and kissed me and made me feel at home from the moment I arrived.

"I realized that it would be difficult at home in the summer. Dad and Mother would do everything possible to try to get me to change my mind about marrying Clarence. My mind couldn't be changed, but I didn't want to be around them while they were acting so narrow-mindedly. I hadn't fallen in love with the appearance of a man; I had fallen in love with the man himself. I applied to graduate school and was accepted. My grades the last two years were strong, so I was able to get a partial scholarship. I took a summer job to earn the rest of my tuition. I didn't want to ask my parents for anything. During that period, I lived with a sorority sister who was from the D.C. area. Her parents had an extra room and since the arrangement wouldn't be indefinite, they were happy to have me.

"In December, Clarence and I flew to Martinique for our wedding and honeymoon. My father agreed to pay the wedding expenses, as he should have, and he and Mother came for the ceremony. They arrived the morning of it and left right after the reception. My father's parting words to me that day were, 'I came to give you away and that's exactly what I've done.' That was the last time I saw either of them."

Joan had a lot to take in. She wanted to be certain that she understood correctly. "You mean that your parents dislike Dad because he is —." Joan could not finish. The idea was still too absurd to her, even after her talks with her father and some of the reading she had done at his suggestion. Then everything became crystal clear. Now she viewed her mother in a different light. She was not the carefree, sometimes insensitive person she appeared. She had been deeply hurt herself. In trying to protect Joan, she had sometimes been the very cause of that pain. Kitty's parents had expected things of her because she was light-skinned. Kitty, however, saw more deeply than skin color.

"Because he is too dark," Kitty finished Joan's unended sentence. "In all of the letters and phone calls that Mother made to me before the wedding, she kept telling me I must reconsider. Clarence wasn't my type, she said. When that didn't work, she finally said that I should think about my children. That really did it. I told her that as for *our* children, Clarence would make a wonderful father and I would be a loving mother, no matter what color my children were." At that point, Kitty looked directly at Joan. "Well?" she asked.

"Well, what?"

"Have I been a loving mother? I know Clarence is the kind of father that I predicted."

Joan took her mother's hands into her own and squeezed them gently, then answered honestly, "Most of the time. Most of the time."

The luncheon over, Joan and her mother completed their shopping. By the end of the spree a dress had been purchased so an additional trip was unneeded.

School ended. Joan, Betsy, and their parents started at once to enjoy the change of pace. Betsy went off to Union Pier for two weeks and returned with just a slight tan, much to the delight of Kitty Williams. Next Joan's parents were to go to the Bahamas. The Bakers, the couple who would watch over the girls, were so enthusiastic about this chance that Kitty and Clarence decided to extend their vacation and visit Kitty's parents in New Orleans before returning to Chicago.

Chapter 14

During her parents' absence Joan, occupied herself by making sure that everything for the party was ready. The guest list was the most difficult matter. To that she would have to give her utmost attention. Hoping that inspiration would eventually come, Joan settled down to reading. She reacquainted herself with some old favorites. *Rebecca* and *Jamaica Inn* were among those. *The Scarlet Pimpernel* was new for her. Struck by his daring-do, she decided to take a bold step also.

It had been a long time since she had talked to Bernie. They had passed each other in the school corridors with a friendly nod and an occasional "How's everything?" She knew that he would never make the first move toward a reconciliation. Maybe they could pick up where they left off. Buoying herself with thoughts of a happy ending, she dialed Bernie's number. Although months had gone by since she last used it, she still remembered his phone number. That must portend something favorable, she thought. On the third ring she heard Bernie's voice. Her positive resolve melted, but she decided she could not just hang up. "Hello, Bernie. This —"

"Hi, Joan," he said before she could give her name. *Another good omen*, she thought.

"Yes, this is Joan. How's everything?" She could have slapped her own face. She had not called to see how trite she could sound.

"OK. How are things with you?" he said, hitting the ball squarely back into her court.

"I'm planning a birthday party and —"

"You wanted me to do the napkins." he laughed.

"No, Bernie. That's not why I called. I wondered if you'd be interested in coming. It's been such a long time since we've really seen each other and I thought this'd be an ideal time."

"Hey, that's great. And you know, I still haven't figured out that movie, but I've had it on my mind.

"*Last Year at Marienbad*," she almost whispered. "I've thought about it, too," she said, picking up his lead. "I've got some ideas about it now," she lied. "I think if I saw it once more I'd have it completely figured out."

"Same old Joanie," he responded. "Still smart as ever."

"Come off it. What's this smart stuff. I'm just a hard worker."

"Yeah, and a hard woman. I bet you'll go far."

"I didn't call to talk about all of that. I called to invite you to my sweet sixteen party. It'll be next month, but I personally wanted to ask my special friends. Of course, I'll send out invitations as well."

"Joanie, it's really great that you called. I really do appreciate it and I don't see why I won't be able to come. In fact, I'm looking forward to it."

"Good, and maybe we'll see each other before then," she added before hanging up.

Joan almost jumped for joy. It was not as difficult as she had imagined. Now that she had her own date for the party, she could decide on her other guests. She wanted to have a few more boys than girls. She also did not want her party to conflict with someone else's. Thinking hard, she could not recall an organized party that early in August. She would be ahead of the back-to-school festivities. This time there would be no French phrases— just a direct, "You're invited to Joan Williams' Sixteenth Birthday Party, Eight until Midnight."

The telephone rang in the midst of Joan's mental planning.

"Hi, Joanie; it's Bernie."

"Hi, Bernie," she giggled.

"I want to ask you a couple of things."

"Sure. Ask away."

"What would you like for your birthday? Sixteen is a special age. I'd like to get you something nice."

"Gee, I don't know. Maybe a necklace of some sort."

"Good. That'll give me something to go on."

"You said there were a couple of things you wanted to ask. That's only one."

"Yeah. I wanted to know if I could bring Trish to your party. She and I are going together. I think you know her. She's captain of the cheerleaders."

The phone suddenly became very hot in Joan's hand. Her ear burned and tears swelled up in her eyes and her throat contracted. Of course she knew Trish. Everyone knew tall, pretty Trish. She was one of the most popular girls at Hyde Park. "Sure, it's alright. I guess I didn't make it clear that the invitation was for you and your date.

"Thanks, Joanie. We'll see you in August. I'll look for the invitation and set that night aside."

Joan's tears fell in full force once she replaced the receiver. She had been writing her name and Bernie's name on a piece of paper while thinking about her party. Ironically, where she had written "Bernie and Joan," it was the "Joan" that had been smeared by her tears. "Bernie" was still intact in bold, black strokes.

Chapter 15

The hot, humid, Chicago summer dragged on. Joan tried not to become overanxious about her party, but it was never very far from her thoughts. The slightest thing could make her think of August. A floral arrangement, a magazine cover, a popular song- -just about everything suggested the party to her.

Her parents returned and were full of news about New Orleans. It seemed that Dr. Williams was much more acceptable than Mr. Williams had been. Kitty's parents were able to see that the marriage was a successful one and attitudes were, after all, changing. It was now comfortable for the DuPuis's to introduce Clarence into their society. He was intelligent, urbane, accomplished, and above all, he truly loved Kitty. All things considered, they were able to feel themselves very fortunate. Not all of their friends could boast an identical claim.

As part of the reconciliation, all of the Williamses would travel to New Orleans for an authentic Creole Thanksgiving. Joan was not sure what that would entail, but she knew she would enjoy it.   However excited Kitty and Clarence were about the turn of events, they knew Joan would be eager to share her own news. As soon as Clarence and Kitty concluded, Joan was asked about the party plans.

"How did you progress with the party details? I really missed not being here to help you," said Kitty.

"Everything more or less is ready. No one is planning anything the night of my party. And the kids I've talked to seem genuinely excited about coming."

"Did you get your whole guest list done?"

"Just about.   I've put forty names on it, although I know all of them won't be able to come no matter what they say now."

"Let's see your list."   It was Joan's father speaking now.

Joan excused herself and went to her room to get the list. All of the party preparations were meticulously recorded in a large, divided notebook. Turning to the section entitled "Guests," she handed the book to her father. He carefully studied the names. Occasionally he uttered a grunt of approval. Sometimes there was a sound that was impossible to categorize.   A few times he just raised his eyebrows. When he finished his perusal, he said, "I have just one question."

"What's that, Dad?"

"Why are there so many boys on the list? It looks as though two-thirds of the names are guys. Why is that?"

"At my last party there wasn't as much dancing as I'd hoped for because there were too few boys. This time I'm trying to make it easier for dancing. I was even hoping that you'd let us roll up the rugs in the living room so there'll be plenty of room for dancing."

"I should say so. You'll have to see that the wood floor is highly polished to protect it."

Kitty looked at the other sections of the book. When she returned it to Joan, Joan asked her mother what she thought.

"Joan, I think you're going to have a lovely party. Everything down to the smallest detail has been accounted for," she answered, beaming at Joan.

Joan was certainly happy to have her mother's praise and her father's approval. But she was not as confident as her mother that all the details had been taken care of. Nevertheless, Joan endured the few remaining weeks wishing that somehow things would work themselves out. As the date for the party grew nearer, she lost even more of her confidence. There was some small consolation in knowing that her party would probably be well attended, even if she did not have a special fellow of her own.

Finally the day of her party arrived. Everything was as ready as it could ever be. The caterer would come one hour before the affair to set up the food, punch, and cake. The parquet floors shone enticingly with a mirror-like brightness. The records were ready. Most of them belonged to Joan. The others were borrowed from her school lockermate, Suzanna. To make sure that none of the records had to leave early, Joan invited Suzanna to spend the night.

Joan had been experimenting with her cosmetics and was able to make herself look quite attractive. She blended the colors of her foundation and the effect was one that enhanced her rich complexion. For this occasion, she clipped a picture from *Ebony Magazine* of a hairstyle she liked. Joan was being sent to Kitty's beautician for this event.

"Joan, hurry up. Raymond doesn't like to be kept waiting," Kitty called from in front of the apartment.

"OK. I'm coming," yelled Joan as she gathered her picture, cosmetics, and the book about Sojourner Truth she was currently reading.

"Mother, do you think I ought to have a manicure, too?"

"It's your day. Why not? But ask them not to cut your cuticles and select a soft color nail polish," was Kitty's advice.

Just as Kitty closed the door to their apartment, the phone rang. "Darn it," she said as she fumbled for her keys. "Joan, go to the car. I'll be right down."

Kitty reached the telephone and said somewhat impatiently as she spoke into it, "Yes?"

"Aunt Kitty?" The voice was unsure.

"Oh, dear. How are you?"

"I'm fine, but I've been waiting in Union Station for about an hour —"

"You're in town? Oh, goodness. I didn't know when you were coming."

"I guess you didn't get my postcard. I dropped a note to let you know when I'd get to Chicago. Mother told me to call you before I left my friend's house. I made a stop along the way. Looks like I should have done what Mother said."

"Listen, I'll be right down to get you. I've just got to drop Joan off at the beauty shop and then I'll come for you."

"I can take a cab if it's easier."

"No, no. I'll be there directly. I hope you have some party clothes because we're having a big one here tonight. I'll tell you all about that later. See you in a little bit," she said as she replaced the phone and dashed out to the car.

"Joan, your cousin is here from New Orleans. Well, a distant cousin actually. I should have let you extend the invitation to your party, but I went ahead and did it. I hope that's alright with you and that you two hit it off."

"What's one person more or less? Of course it's alright." But what she was thinking was, *That's all I need now. A pretty cousin from New Orleans. Well, maybe she'll offer Trish some competition.*

Kitty pulled up in front of Raymond's Beauty Salon. Joan quickly got out of the car and walked into the shop as though she were used to such luxury. "I'm Joan Williams," she said to the receptionist. "I have a ten-thirty appointment with Raymond. I'd also like to have a manicure."

"Certainly, Miss Williams," was the friendly reply. "I'll have Sally do your nails while you're under the dryer."

At that point Raymond escorted an elderly blue-rinsed lady to the reception area. The blue-rinse was beaming at the way she looked. "Thank you, Raymond. You always know what to do."

Raymond nodded ever so slightly and said, "Take care, Mrs. Witherspoon. We'll see you next Saturday." Then to Joan, "Miss Williams, I believe. You can come back now."

Chapter 16

Joan showed Raymond the picture of the hair-style she wanted to copy. He approved but suggested soft bangs to replace the more pronounced side-sweep. "After all, Joan, you want to look sixteen, not twenty-six."

While Raymond worked, Joan became more confident of his skill. She, therefore, ventured to ask about her makeup. She told him how she experimented and explained the look she wanted to achieve.

"Did you bring your cosmetics with you?" he inquired.

"Yes, I have them in this bag."

"Before I comb you out, put your makeup on and I'll frame your hair around your face. Then if adjustments have to be made, we can do it at that time."

"I'm having a manicure, too."

"Good. You'll want a clear polish and, of course, you'll want your cuticles pushed back, not cut."

"That's right. I don't want my cuticles cut and a clear polish will be fine."

Two and one-half hours later, Joan was on the phone to let her mother know that she was ready to be taken home. "Good-bye, Raymond. And thank you," she called as she left the shop. As she entered her family's car, she saw her cousin for the first time. Kitty was making polite introductions, but neither Joan nor Chris heard what she was saying. They were speaking a private, silent language with their eyes.

To Chris, Joan looked picture perfect. Soft, dark hair gently framed her face. A subtle pastel green colored the areas around her large, brown eyes. There was just a hint of pink at the cheeks and lips and the skin was smooth and flawless. Joan was beautiful, poised, and cool. Chris certainly had not expected this.

Joan was simultaneously summing up her cousin. The height was hard to judge from a seated position, but Joan guessed that Chris was taller than average. The complexion underneath the summer tan was probably fair. The hair was somewhere between brown and auburn and was sun-streaked. As the clouds covered and uncovered the sun, the color of Chris's eyes appeared to change, but the dominant color was unmistakably green. The total effect was dazzling. Joan had definitely not expected this.

Kitty could not help but feel the electricity in the air. At last she managed to say something that caught their attention.

"Would you repeat what you just said, Aunt Kitty?"

"I said, you're cousins over three times removed."

"That means we aren't really related, except for a probable common ancestor way back when, that is," said Chris.

"That's what I was explaining. That as well as how it slipped my mind that Laverne had asked about your coming for a visit." The rest of the ride home continued in silence. Kitty pulled up in front of their building then, remembering her need to get some gas, let Chris and Joan out and said she would be back shortly.

On the way up the stairs, Joan reopened the conversation. "Chris, I'm having a few friends over this evening for my sixteenth birthday. Would you like to join us?"

"I was hoping you would ask. Yes, I'd like that very much." As Joan was putting the key in the apartment door, Chris added, "Do you have a guy you're going to be with tonight?"

"No. Everyone's just school friends," she said, thinking briefly of Bernie.

"In that case, may I reserve the first dance?" he said but meant much more.

"Yes," answered Joan, meaning infinitely more herself.

Once inside they each went to attend to their own needs. Joan's concern was the party. Chris had to unpack and went out a few times. The caterers arrived and set up. By 7:30 everything was ready. Suzanna came at 7:45 with her promised records and her overnight case. By five minutes to eight, Joan's guests began to arrive. They came in almost a steady stream and by 8:20 everyone, including Bernie and Trish, was there. Everyone except Chris. Dancing had started but nobody had yet asked Joan to dance. At 8:30 the doorbell rang. Joan, who was talking with a small group of girls, excused herself.

Opening the door, she discovered Chris. He took her firmly by the hand and led her into the dining room. He then took out the corsage he was hiding behind his back and expertly pinned the orchid onto Joan's pale pink dress. Everyone, including the dancers, stopped to watch. Just as Chris finished pinning the flower on, he said softly, yet loudly enough for all to hear, "Happy sweet sixteen." Then he firmly kissed her on the lips and claimed his dance.

After that dance, Joan's guests suddenly remembered the reason for the party. They seemed also to notice her for the first time. Bernie came up to tell her how wonderful she looked. "Joan you look beautiful tonight. Happy birthday, and I have something for you." He reached into his pocket and withdrew a small, prettily wrapped package and handed it to her.

Joan took the box, started to open it, but found that her hands were trembling. She handed the gift back to Bernie and said, "Would you open it for me?"

Bernie obliged.   Under the pink and white paper was a small, white box. Inside the box was a gold chain with a dainty cross on it. Bernie held it up for all to see.

"It's beautiful. Will you fasten it around my neck?"

Bernie placed the chain around her bare neck and fastened the clasp. Now everyone in the crowd was watching Bernie and Joan. Someone said, "Doesn't she look fantastic!" Trish could not help but hear the remark. The whole room heard it. Trish decided it was time for her to reclaim Bernie. Joan was getting ample attention. She did not need more of Bernie's, but before she could reach Bernie, someone had put the music back on and Bernie and Joan were dancing.

Trish waited until the record was over but was at Bernie's elbow when the tune ended. "Great party, Joan," she said, as she ushered Bernie away.

Throughout the evening all the male guests danced with Joan at least once. Just before midnight Chris took it upon himself to announce, "It's midnight. Time for the last dance. Get your partner." Chris already had Joan by the hand even as he was speaking. Somebody had turned down the rheostat to its lowest setting so the room was practically dark. The lighted controls from the stereo unit were the brightest lights in the room. Chris and Joan danced to the haunting strains of *Smoke Gets In Your Eye*s and whenever Chris thought they were hidden by the shadows, nibbled playfully on Joan's earlobe and neck. Frequently his mouth sought hers and just as frequently found it.

Joan could not believe that all of this was happening to her. Her party was a greater success than she could have hoped for. The unpleasant memories from her Christmas party were almost erased. Joan was definitely the brightest star this night. She literally shone as she savored the attention being lavished upon her. It was palatable. She could taste it just as she could taste Chris's kisses. She liked the deliciousness of every moment. She had never felt this way about any boy before.

New feelings were awakening in her. Chris's body against hers as they danced caused her to feel —. She found it hard to put these sensations into words that were uniquely her own. She tingled all over. Her heart beat faster and louder. She was breathless and lightheaded.

Her eyes, which had been closed during this last dance, now opened. She looked straight into her mother's eyes but could not read their expression because the rest of Kitty's face was hidden by her husband's shoulder. Evidently her parents had come in for the last dance. She was not sure how long they had been in the room or what they had observed.

As last the strains of the tune came to an end, someone turned up the rheostat, and the dull glow became a bright glare. The guests began to depart, some in single file, some in pairs, but most in small groups. When Bernie and Trish approached the door, Bernie paused and said, "It was really a nice party. Happy birthday." He bent down as if to place a kiss on Joan's forehead. Before he was able to complete the movement, Trish stepped between him and Joan, extended her right hand to Joan and said, "Thanks for a swell evening. Bernie and I had a very nice time. We'll probably see you when school starts. Enjoy the rest of the summer." With that, Trish took Bernie's hand and walked him out of the door.

By twelve-twenty all the party-goers had left. Only Chris and Suzanna remained. Suzanna said, "That was a great party, Joan. I don't know when I've danced so much. Do you want me to help you clean up?"

As Joan surveyed the situation, she saw that the caterers had carefully put everything back in place. Now they were folding the tablecloth and in a few minutes would depart. There was nothing left to be done, and Joan's parents were eager to get everyone settled for the night.

"Joan, you and Suzanna had better get off to bed. I know you'll be awake half the night talking and will be sleepy heads in the morning," said Joan's mother.

"There's not much left of the night," said Joan's father as he glanced at his watch. With that he kissed his daughter on the cheek and whispered, "Good night, sweet sixteen."

Chris, who had been in the kitchen, came into the dining room in the midst of the good nights. "Oh," said Kitty, turning around, "I thought you'd already gone to bed."

"Just getting a glass of milk. Now I'm off."

Everybody left the dining room and headed down the corridor. Kitty and Clarence came to their room first. Joan and Suzanna were next and turned into Joan's bedroom. Chris was last to arrive at his. The curious arrangement of rooms that had so intrigued Joan had become guest quarters. Light could be seen peeping from under the doors of each person's room. Then, one by one, the lights went out. Kitty was last to turn off her light and as she did she sighed.

Chapter 17

Suzanna was eager to talk about the events of the evening. She did not care that the room was in darkness. Joan feigned tiredness and said they would talk in the morning. Joan, however, was far from being tired or sleepy. She needed time to sift through and properly sort out her own feelings. *How did I feel when Bernie and Trish came in?* she wondered. *Jealous?* No, she decided that anxious more aptly described the feeling. *But anxious about what?* She had known Bernie would be bringing Trish so that was no surprise. Perhaps she was anxious about herself. Yes, that was it. She did not want Bernie to feel sorry for her. One year they had found solace in each other's company. Now the situation had changed. He certainly did not need her. By dating Trish, he had done what Joan had yet to accomplish. He had been accepted by the group and Joan was still on the outside. But more importantly, Bernie had someone and Joan wanted someone.

That line of reasoning brought her directly to Chris. Was it Chris she wanted or was he just the "someone" necessary to her at this time? Next she tried to analyze her feelings for him. He was handsome, sure of himself, a good dancer, and he knew how to make a girl feel like a woman. But what else did she know about him? And did she dare investigate? Concluding that even Sherlock Holmes with his cool, calculating, incisiveness might require more than fourteen hours to unravel something as complex as the human character, Joan drifted off into an uneasy sleep, alternately seeing Bernie's face and hearing his voice but unable to make out what he was saying and feeling Chris' moist kisses as he explored her body.

The morning dawned bright, hot, and humid. Fortunately there was a breeze blowing off Lake Michigan. Having forgotten to lower the window shades, Joan and Suzanna awakened earlier that they had planned. Sensing that they were the only ones awake in the house, they were able to indulge in the overdue tete-a-tete.

Suzanna stretched her cream-colored arms toward the ceiling, suppressed a yawn, and started talking almost in one movement. "That was some party, Joan. You and Chris really put on quite a show."

"What do you mean?" said Joan with alarm in her voice.

"Oh, you know," teased Suzanna.

"But I don't know. Tell me what you mean."

"I mean you, the two sides of you. There's the quiet, studious Joan that we all know and there's

Joan the siren whose song was heard loud and clear last night. But he's some kind of guy. I don't blame you in the least. I'd give anything for a chance at him."

"But Chris was the one coming on so strong. I was —"

"You were eating it up," continued her friend. "But as I said, I don't blame you. After all, what could you do with Bernie having the nerve to bring that Trish character after all you and he have been through."

Joan was sorry now that she had confided in Suzanna. Yet she had to have someone to talk to. "You think I put on a show for Bernie's sake? He's a finished book. He's been on the shelf for a long time. We're really just friends."

"Well, that may be so, but everyone at school thought Bernie dropped you because you weren't —oh, you know. You were too goody goody."

"I see. But I'm sure you set everyone straight."

Now it was Suzanna's turn to squirm. But she was quick and said, "You bet I did. I told them that you and Bernie more or less consented to drift apart. And after tonight, no one can doubt that."

"And now what is that supposed to mean?" demanded Joan as she tried to keep from losing her temper.

"I mean that your Goody Two Shoes image is a bust and that now you seem more with it."

"Oh. I see. I'm just one of the girls now. Is that it?"

"Joan, take it easy. What I'm saying doesn't lessen you in anyone's eyes. It's just that most of us thought of you solely as a bookworm. You can seem so aloof. Sometimes even I can't figure you out. We didn't realize that you had time for real feelings. Now we see that you have other interests as well. Don't worry. It's alright. It's natural to like boys. It's okay to show it."

"If any damage has been done, I guess I have only myself to blame," said a calmer Joan.

"Joan! Have you heard anything I've been saying? Your halo hasn't fallen off. Not that I would worry about that anyway. It's just now we see you as a normal girl who just happens to be smart."

Joan was somewhat relieved by Suzanna's last remarks. She was not positive she agreed with everything that had been said. A reputation is a valuable thing. She knew her father would have a great deal to say on that topic. She knew her mother felt that impressions and appearances were important. Joan would have to rethink many of the points her friend had made. Right now she thought it only fair to inquire about Suzanna's evening. What Suzanna shared paled in comparison to Joan's night. Nevertheless, Suzanna had enjoyed the dancing and was happy to have slept over. Temporarily talked out, the two girls lay down once more and slept a few hours longer.

Chapter 18

Chris, normally an early riser, made no exception this first full morning in his aunt's house. "Distant aunt," he kept reminding himself. Each morning prior to eating breakfast, he performed thirty minutes of calisthenics- running in place, deep knee bends, sit-ups and push-ups. These exercises cleared his mind and also, he liked to think, kept him more closely attuned to nature. This morning, after the party, it was the clearing of his mind that mattered most. He had hoped that he had not scared Joan off. She seemed so innocent, so likable, and so vulnerable. When he first made his move, he felt that she had shied away from his advances. But by the last kiss, he was sure she had responded, even if just a little bit.

At the end of his allotted thirty minutes, Chris was not sure he had accomplished his twin goals. He took a cool shower quickly because he thought he was the only one awake and did not want to disturb the household with the sound of running water. After his shower he walked to the study to look for something to read. He wanted to remove himself from his current situation for the moment. Selecting a back issue of *Field and Stream* he settled down with it.

Kitty and Clarence awakened early also. Upon first arising, Kitty crept down the long hallway and looked in on Betsy who was fast asleep in her darkened room.   When Kitty paused at Joan's room, she could hear the girls' voices. *Still talking about the party, no doubt*, she thought as she continued toward the last set of rooms.   From it she heard the sound of Chris running in place.   She was glad she had carpeted that floor.   She certainly did not want her neighbors disturbed.

When Kitty returned to her bedroom, Clarence was sitting up with the night stand lamp on.   He had the suggestion of a grin on his face but said nothing.   He waited for Kitty to open the conversation as he knew she would.   Living with Kitty for almost eighteen years had taught him a great deal about her.   She climbed back into bed, stared at the ceiling for a few minutes, and then began. "Do you think it'll be alright?"

"What's that, dear?"

"Joan and Chris, as if you hadn't noticed."

"Of course, they'll be alright.   We've raised a bright but sensible young woman.   That's exactly what she is now, a young woman.   She's exploring and expanding her horizons, but she won't lose her way," Clarence reassured his wife.

"I do hope you're right."

"I am."

"But she wasn't like this with Bernie," Kitty persisted.

"We really don't know how she was with Bernie. At any rate, she wasn't sixteen then. She's growing up."

"Yes, you're probably right." Curling up next to Clarence, Kitty gave in, kissed her husband, and went back to sleep.

A couple of hours later the aroma of a morning meal pervaded the apartment. The smell of freshly brewing coffee was dominant, but there was a hint of eggs, pancakes, and warming maple syrup. As the house was being scented, those who were still asleep awakened most pleasantly. By ten, just as Kitty was setting a large pitcher of freshly squeezed orange juice on the table in the solarium which also served as a summer breakfast room, Betsy, the last of the sleepyheads, found her way to a seat at the table. From the dining room drifted the sounds of a rousing church hymn.

"Aren't we going to church today?" asked Betsy by way of a greeting.

"We'll miss this Sunday. But we can hear a service over the radio," said her father. Everyone was politely quiet and listened to the sermon as they ate breakfast. When the program was over the solemn atmosphere dissolved.

Betsy, who had missed the party because of her age, wanted to know how it went and how it felt to be sixteen. To an eight-year-old, sixteen was a lifetime away.

Joan filled her in on the details that she wanted her to know and concluded by saying that all the guests said they had enjoyed themselves. Chris volunteered that if everyone had only half the fun he had, it would still have been a success. Suzanna echoed Chris' sentiments.

After these comments the conversation did not know where to take itself. A few things were said about the delicious breakfast. The juice was praised as much as orange juice can be. Then each fell into concentrating deeply on the rest of their meal.

Joan was trying hard to seem as normal as possible, but her efforts at giving all her attention to her food were hampered by the feeling that she was being stared at. Tired of averting her eyes from the probable source of that feeling, she looked up and saw that she had been correct. Chris' green eyes were looking directly into her brown ones. His expression was playful. Joan was not sure whether that was so because he liked the view or that he enjoyed the discomfort he was causing her.

"Joan, what are your plans for the rest of the day? I'd like to go to the Museum of Science and Industry. There are some exhibits I've read about that I'd like to see. If you and Suzanna and Betsy are interested, perhaps we could give your folks a break and clear out for awhile," said Chris.

Suzanna looked at Joan for a clue as to what her response should be, but received no help. So she said, hesitantly, "I think perhaps I'd better be getting home."

Betsy, on the other hand, was pleased to be included and said without reluctance, "I'd like to go. I always want to see Colleen Moore's doll house. When are we leaving?

"It's settled then," said Chris. "We'll go at noon. Why don't you reconsider, Suzanna? If you don't have to go home, come with us."

It was a happy Suzanna who said, "Alright. I can spend a few more hours away from home."

The youngsters left the table to go to their rooms to prepare for the museum. All but Betsy took extreme care in dressing. Suzanna had only brought one change of clothing, but she spent as much time as Joan putting herself together.

Clarence offered Chris the use of the car and said Joan could provide directions. The museum was only a short ride from their house so he was not worried about Chris and traffic problems.

When they arrived at their destination, Betsy wanted to see the doll house right away. "I don't think you should go off alone," said Chris. "Suzanna, why don't you go with Betsy and we'll meet at the —"

"At the coal mine entrance," supplied Joan.

"Good. We'll meet at the coal mine entrance in, say, an hour," said Chris. That taken care of, Betsy and Suzanna went off in the direction of the doll house while Chris, with Joan in tow, went to ask directions to the exhibits he had come to see.

Chris thanked the museum guide and then turned to Joan to ask if there was a place to grab a cold drink before seeing the exhibits.

Joan took them to the museum's cafeteria, found a clear place, and waited for Chris to bring their beverages. "Joan," he began, "there isn't too much time, but I want to get things straight about last night."

She knew what was coming. Upon more careful reflection he had changed his mind. Things always looked different in the light of day.

"I shouldn't have come on the way I did last night and I don't want you to get the wrong impression," he continued.

Now he's trying to cushion the blow. He's letting me down easily, she reflected as Chris talked.

"I like you very much. I know I've only just met you, but sometimes it doesn't take long to realize these things. I want to spend as much time as possible with you before I go back. I guess it's because our time will be limited that I acted as I did last night. Actually, I just got carried away. My father has always told me to act aggressively, to go after anything I felt was worthwhile. I hope by applying that philosophy to you I didn't damage any chance I might have had."

"Chris, I think you're trying to apologize for your behavior last night. Why don't we just start all over and get to know one another? Well?"

"Joan, you're wonderful. Okay. Here goes. I'm Christopher Louis LaSalle. I'll be entering my third year at Wilberforce where I'll be majoring in engineering.   My dad's an engineer in New Orleans, as was his father. We have our own company.   I recently turned twenty and up until last night, I've only been involved with girls my own age or older.   I'm not trying to rush you into anything you can't or don't want to handle. But I like you; I want to be with you and go on from there. Now, tell me about yourself in twenty-five words or less."

They both laughed. Then Joan briefly told him about herself. She told him about her loneliness. This she had not meant to do, but it just poured out on its own. Instead of regretting what had slipped out, she felt relieved.

"Joan, you've paid me a great compliment. You've trusted me with your secret. Now I'll trust you with mine. If I don't write a fantastic paper and remove an incomplete from my record, I'm going to be in serious trouble at school, not to mention what my dad'll do to me."

"Does this have anything to do with our being at the museum?"

"Go to the head of the class."

"Well, we've got forty-five minutes before we're to meet my sister and Suzanna. Let's get started. Where to first?"

Chris heard the "we" and knew that Joan was in his corner. Things were going to work out for him, he felt sure. Off they went to see the first exhibition.

Their time was soon up and they went to meet the others at the coal mine. Suzanna and Betsy were a little late in coming. Chris purchased four tickets for the coal mine ride and arranged with Joan for several additional trips to the museum. She suggested other sources of information and wondered aloud if she might be able to get her father to check out some books from the University of Chicago's library for Chris to use.

The two girls showed up before long and they all went on the next coal mine ride. As they traveled into the bowels of the darkened mine in authentic coal cars, Joan and Chris were quite naturally thrown against one another during the course of the bumpy ride. Chris had already been sitting close to Joan, but at every joust he seemed to get nearer yet.

A general meandering around the museum completed their outing. When they returned to Joan's father's car, she suggested a most indirect route home. She asked Chris to drive to the west side. She wanted to see her old neighborhood. Why she could not have said. Betsy confessed to not remembering much about where they lived even though only a couple of years had passed. Joan proved to be a capable navigator and directed them there and back without difficulty. She did not know what she had expected, but what she discovered was that the west side held no attraction for her whatever. It was not home anymore. The drive back to Hyde Park was a welcome one.

Chapter 19

Suzanna packed her overnight case and gathered her records to return home once they got back. Chris offered to take her home if Joan's dad did not mind his using the car again. When Chris returned, Betsy filled everyone's head with her impressions of the doll house. After dinner, Chris, Betsy, and Kitty watched television. Joan and her father found the quiet of the study for a talk.

"Joan, is there anything in particular you want to discuss? We haven't done this in some time, but I don't think I'm too rusty," he said.

"As a matter of fact, I do want to talk about something specific. I want to talk about Chris and how I feel about him, or at least how I think I feel about him."

"Let's hear it."

"I'm not sure where to begin. But first, just how closely related are we?"

Her father laughed, not at her but in a way that eased the tension. "According to your mother you're distant cousins over five times removed. Except for genealogical purposes, you two aren't related at all. Your mother is from an old family and they like to know how everyone fits in. If you listen to her, the whole of New Orleans can be included in her family. For all I know, you could be more related to Bernie than to Chris."

"That's what I thought- not about Bernie, about Chris."

"No, Chris is just a friend of your mother's family. That's all. Out of politeness and custom, they refer to one another as aunt and nephew and cousin and the like."

"Well, that brings me to the next question. Is he too old for me? He's already twenty and in college.

"That," said her father "is a more difficult question to answer. Chris is older than you and he is in college. No doubt he's experienced more of life than you have. And he's probably had an easy time with the ladies. But you have to look deeper than that and you have to look into yourself as well.

"He says he likes me and I'm definitely attracted by him. I see something substantial beneath his good looks and smooth manner."

"I think," continued Joan's father, "that the next question has to be put to you. Can you handle him and not compromise your own integrity?"

"It's like you've given me all the pieces of a puzzle, but I have to make a picture out of them myself."

"I couldn't have put it better."

From there they moved to other topics and before the conversation ended, Joan had secured her father's assistance with the books for Chris without giving away his secret.

Although the others had been paying attention to the program they were watching, they knew an important conference was being held behind the closed doors of the study. All were relieved when father and daughter emerged smiling and joined them in front of the television set.

As the final days of the summer advanced, Joan and Chris established a routine of sorts. When they were not going around to engineering exhibits, they were in the library amassing notes and copying diagrams. The books her father secured for Chris were of value, too. Joan helped Chris organize his paper into a clear, precise piece of writing. Joan's father's secretary, always eager for extra work, was paid to type it and the finished product was more than Chris had hoped for. He knew quite well that it would be accepted and that it would receive a very high, if not the top mark.

When they were not working on his paper, Joan and Chris found time to take in a play. This impressed Joan because she had only been taken to a movie on her single date with Bernie. Her parents had taken her to some seasonal productions at the Goodman Theatre, but going to the theater with a young man was a totally different experience. She and Chris also went to see one of the free concerts in Grant Park. They even went to some of the parties the Hyde Parkers gave as summer vacation drew to its close.

During their moments alone together, Chris never pushed Joan to handle anything she was not ready for. His kisses were passionate, but whenever his hands began to explore, Joan gently took them and pressed his fingers to her lips. He understood her unspoken signal, but he never stopped trying.

Almost three weeks to the day of his arrival, Chris prepared for his return to New Orleans. He would spend a little time at his home and then he would go back to Wilberforce. He and Joan exchanged promises to write, and at the train station they had some last words.

"Joan, I'll call you when I get home and here's a little something for you. Don't open it until you get home."

Joan took a book-sized box from his hands. *It's not very heavy— just about the right weight for a volume of love poems*, she thought.

"Thanks, Chris. It's been a wonderful summer. I really enjoyed every minute of your visit."

"And don't forget about October. I'm expecting you." With that last remark, he kissed her firmly but briefly on the mouth. He thanked his "aunt" and "uncle" for their hospitality. Then he bent down, brushed Betsy's cheek with his lips, and boarded his train. Its departure was not delayed and in a few minutes, not much could be seen of the train that carried Chris away.

Back in the car, Joan alternately stared at and hugged the package to her. Paying no attention to the drive home, but remembering every detail of the past three weeks, she was amazed to find herself sitting in front of her house with her father holding the car door open.

"That was a quick trip," she said, trying to recover.

"No, it wasn't," countered Betsy. "We were stuck at one traffic light through seven red lights. I counted."

Joan emerged from the car, went upstairs, and then directly to her room. She shut the door and sat down on the side of her bed. Suddenly, warm tears filled her eyes and began making paths that ended on the package she was still clutching. She swayed back and forth as if rocking a baby and moaned, "Chris, Chris, Chris." When the tears stopped, Joan reached for a tissue, wiped her eyes, and looked at her package.

Carefully she removed the paper. Each piece she folded ever so neatly and then opened the white Field's box. Inside the box was a large pink envelope and a smaller box nesting securely with the aid of tissue paper. Opening the envelope first and pulling out a piece of stationery, Joan saw Chris' large, loose scrawl. The message was short and to the point. "Be my girl, completely and always, Love Chris." Putting this aside she opened

the other box which contained a still smaller par-
cel that was kept in place by still more paper.
Inside it was at last what Chris had intended for
her. There was a ring inside, his high school class
ring. As she lifted it out, she discovered that it had
been put on a sturdy, gold chain. She fingered her
neck and removed the cross that Bernie had given
her and placed it in the back of her jewelry box.
She studied Chris' ring, then put the chain around
her neck. As she did she thought, *I knew it was
right. Everything will be fine because he loves me,
too.*

Chris called as promised and Joan told him that
she was wearing his ring. She also said that she
would work on coming to Wilberforce for homecoming and that she would let him know about
that other issue as well. The call ended with an "I
love you" from both parties and promises to write
every week.

Later Kitty asked Joan if she did not think that
she was cutting herself off from the other kids by
wearing Chris' ring. This provided Joan the
chance she was waiting for. She needed to talk to
her mother about this and now was an opportune
time.

"Mother, that's just want the others are to me:
kids. We really don't and never did have much in
common. Chris talked to me about trying to finish
high school early. He says I'm just as mature and
certainly smarter than a lot of the people he knows.
I'm sure there must be some tests I can take and

pass out of my last year. Anyway, he's invited me to Wilberforce for homecoming, and to get a glimpse of campus life. He'd like me to attend Wilberforce next year."

Kitty had not guessed that her comment would release this torrent. Instead of continuing out of the room, she sat down in a chair by the living room window. Before, answering she let her fingers run up and down the velvet arm of the chair for a few seconds. "Let's take one issue at a time. As a straight A student I suppose one might make a case for early graduation. We can talk to Vera Thomas about the particulars. And I, too, think you're mature enough for college. As for homecoming —"

Joan interrupted her mother and told her that the sororities opened their houses for visiting guests and that the housemother would be like a chaperon. She explained that it would mean missing two days of school if she went by train but that she would get the assignments and do the work.

Before the conversation went any further, Joan's father was brought in and told what they had been discussing. It was agreed that Joan would apply for early graduation. There was still enough time to make any adjustments that might be required in Joan's classes. As for attending Wilberforce, Joan's father was not ready to commit himself. Both her parents wanted her to consider Howard University, their alma mater. As for visiting Chris in October for homecoming, it was Joan's father who came to the rescue.

"I think we can work something out for home-coming," he said.

Later Kitty said to Clarence, "Why did you give in so easily?"

"Kitty, you know how often teenagers change their minds. In a few weeks with school in full swing, Chris'll be not only out of sight but out of mind as well."

"I hope you're right."

Chapter 20

Joan went to see her counselor at the very first opportunity. Working out the details for graduating ahead of schedule proved to be a problem. This was not something that was done. Miss Thomas advised Joan to take some advanced placement exams and think about early admission after that. Once she had proven that she was truly belonged in college now, they might work something out. There was also a rush to meet deadlines for applications for certain other national exams that Joan was advised to take in case she did gain early entrance. Joan was wished good luck and invited to come to the guidance office should she need anything.

Joan did encounter some resentment from the senior class she might enter. The senior class as a whole did not welcomed her. Joan's straight A average was likely to be repeated in her final year at Hyde Park. That could make her valedictorian. Those who would have invested four years of hard work wanted a crack at the top spot. A compromise was agreed upon in the event of an early graduation for Joan. If she and another student had identical averages, the honor would be shared and the other student would be allowed to give the first valedictory address. Joan intended to be at the top and sharing that honor was fine with her. Most of the third year students liked the idea of early graduation and wished Joan good luck. Suzanna even added that it gave her a new status, having an almost- senior as a best friend.

The remainder of September quickly passed. Joan missed Chris and kept up her weekly letters. If he did not write as he promised, he did call. Now it was her school work that occupied most of her time. Without officially being a part of it, Joan introduced a new dimension to the senior class. Many of the seniors were inspired to equal or better Joan's standard of excellence. No one as yet could surpass her achievements but competition was beneficial. She stimulated the other students and they her.

Her advanced algebra class was proving to be a real challenge, however. Joan was quick in math and this was proving to be detrimental. Mr. Bosworth, her instructor, insisted that all work be completely shown. Joan found this irritating and time consuming. She knew when her answers were correct and could fully explain how she arrived at them. This was not good enough for Mr. Bosworth. In fact, just last week, he said in front of the whole class, "Miss Williams, if you don't start consistently showing all your work, you won't be getting that A you're so desperately chas-

ing." Joan was mortified by the public warning
and fully intended to show every iota of work. She
had come to far to let this man get in her way.

October brought with it a renewed discussion
of the homecoming trip. When Joan and her parents had last talked, Joan proposed taking three
days off to allow for roundtrip travel by train.
Now her father strenuously objected. That was too
much school to miss for a party. "What I'll do," he
said, "is drive you out on Friday. We'll both miss
school that day. You'll be there in time for the
evening activities and in plenty of time for the big
festivities on Saturday. Sunday you can take the
train back. You might not get much rest, but we'll
have you back in school on Monday."

Because there were greater demands on her
time as a senior, the decision satisfied Joan.
Staying on top of her studies was not that hard, but
she did not want to put herself in the position of
playing "catch up." She definitely did not want
people to get the impression that partying was
more important than school.

As October progressed the fall chill gradually
gave way to winter's cold. Lake Michigan no
longer reflected the sun as brightly as it had. The
wind that blew was becoming stronger and nastier.
Those who studied the signs predicted a long,
harsh winter for Chicago. Joan, however, was not
thinking of weather conditions. She had more
immediate concerns- like what to wear while at
Wilberforce.

With her mother's assistance, Joan thoroughly combed her wardrobe. An hour after beginning the task, the two had quite a number of items spread across the bedroom. Some skirts were on the bed and four pairs of shoes lined the floor beside it. Blouses and sweaters smothered a chair.

"Well, what do you think, Joan? Can we pull something together from this?"

"Doing that would be like pulling a rabbit out of a hat. I want to look really outstanding. People are going to scrutinize me."

"That's true," her mother agreed. "But remember you'll also be there as a graduating senior who is looking the school over. Don't be intimidated."

"Remember that Christmas your parents met Dad for the first time?" Joan inquired.

"You bet I do."

"You said you took your best things to the hotel. You told me how much time and care went into preparing for that dinner. Well, this is just as important to me. I don't want anything to go wrong."

"You're right, Joan. Let's rethink this whole thing."

The two began studying back issues of Joan's fashion magazines. After about an hour of this, something was decided. A shopping trip was needed to round out her clothing. She already owned traditional plaid skirts, sweaters, and button down blouses. Now she would add a blazer, a pair of slacks, and a party dress to what she had to complete her needs.

A few days later Joan met her mother downtown after school. They grabbed a bite to eat at Field's Tea Room and then took the bus to North Michigan Avenue and covered the Magnificent Mile in search of Joan's wardrobe additions. They found everything they were looking for and returned to their Hyde Park home tired and happy.

The week before the trip was interminable. At last it was time to close the school books, pack, and say good-bye. Suzanna called just before Joan left the house to wish her a fine time. "And be sure to give Chris my regards," she added.

"Suzanna, I'll tell Chris hello for you and I won't forget any of the details of the weekend. We'll have a long talk when I get back. Thanks for calling." With that she hung up and bolted out of the door and to the car. She looked up at their living room window and waved to her mother, who was standing there.

Chapter 21

The trip to Ohio was uneventful. Occasionally her father would elaborate upon some historical site. He even made her aware of the background of the name of the school she was going to visit. "Wilberforce," he started, "was named after an English politician and philanthropist who lived during the last half of the eighteenth and first third of the nineteenth centuries. He was an abolitionist who helped set up an organization to abolish slave trade. His group particularly struck out at such trade in the West Indies." He gave her more details of William Wilberforce's life and times, but what impressed her was the easy way in which he made history come alive.

Chris had provided Joan with an excellent map of the school. He had drawn it himself and it was a meticulous piece of craftsmanship. Across the top, in his easily identifiable script, was a playful message: "Hurry, hurry."

Joan's first stop was the Alpha Kappa Alpha Sorority House. She was met by a neatly dressed coed named Gloria. Gloria asked Joan and her father in and introduced them to Mrs. Spriggins, the housemother. "And don't you worry none, Dr. Williams. Your little darlin' is in good hands. Now, here's the phone number of our house. Just call anytime you want."

Much reassured, he was able to say, "Have a good weekend, Joan. I'm going to start back now. I'll stop and rest at one of the motels between here and Chicago. I feel as though I can drive a few more hours yet." He kissed her cheek and departed.

Gloria helped Joan to settle in and gave her a few pointers. "We only let a few outside girls stay in our sorority house. What you do reflects on us. We've got a good reputation and that's the way we'd like to keep it. You're Chris' girlfriend, I know, and you'll be spending a lot of time with him. Then, whatever happens, you'll go home to Chicago while the rest of us remain here. Have fun, but play by the rules and you'll be welcome here anytime."

Joan thought that Gloria knew a great deal about her but decided not to press it. She liked Gloria. She was a pretty girl who had a sense of her own worth- a worth based on something other than good looks. Although Joan was familiar with the schedule of events, she listened patiently as Gloria reviewed it. Tonight there was a dance at the Kappa House. Since Chris was one of the hosts, the girls would walk over to the house and meet their dates there. After the dance broke up, about an hour would remain until everyone had to be back at the sorority house. Gloria related all of this information, not as a lecture, but as conversation as both girls dressed for the dance. Joan selected a plaid skirt, tailored blouse, and V-neck sweater. She was grateful to see Gloria similarly attired. At ten minutes to eight they joined other girls. Gloria made introductions and they all headed for the fraternity house.

Before long Joan and her companions reached the Kappa House, which was splendidly decorated in red and white. Joan wanted to take a longer look, but she was ushered in the door along with the other girls, who were more interested in getting inside. Chris and Joan spotted each other simultaneously. He rushed over to greet her and to thank Gloria for letting Joan room with her. Gloria nodded her acknowledgement and went on to find her own date.

Chris and Joan danced, brought each other up to date on local news, and found themselves stared at throughout the evening. "Why," asked Joan, "are people looking at us so hard?"

"I think it's because the word is out that you may be examining us."

"And just how did that happen?

"I think I might have said something about this dynamic person I met over the summer. And then one thing led to another," Chris responded.

"But you didn't tell anyone about-?"

"No, of course not," he said before she could finish. He sensed the alarm in her voice and whispered, "Of course not. No one knows about you skipping your senior year. No one knows how young you are. If they did, they'd accuse me of robbing the cradle."

Joan had spent as much time dressing for this evening as she had for her birthday party. Again, the time spent was woth it. Though Gloria was easily the prettiest girl in the room, it was Joan who was receiving most of the attention. Several of Chris' fraternity brothers came over and asked to be introduced. One even cut in for a dance. Reluctantly Chris gave Joan up. To his friend he said, and not at all in a light-hearted way, "Let's not make a habit of this."

Joan was recording in her mind all that was happening that evening. She had not discerned much difference between high school kids and college kids, at least when they were at a party. It was not until the dance was over and Chris was walking her back to the AKA House that she remembered Suzanna's "hello." Now was hardly the time to be the bearer of messages.

"A penny for your thoughts," Chris said.

"I was just thinking how good it is to be here with you. So much has happened in such a short time. Now a penny for your thoughts."

"I don't know if you'll get your money's worth," Chris began. "I was thinking pretty much the same thing. Last summer I had several problems that needed solving. Everything worked out, in fact, even better than I had reason to hope for because I got you in the bargain."

Although they walked very slowly, they all too quickly found themselves at their destination. Coeds had already begun gathering on the lawn to say their goodnights. Chris looked at Joan and said, "Let's not join that crowd."

Unsure of what he meant, Joan followed as he led her to an alcove several yards away. Either the moon went behind the clouds or the alcove was totally hidden from the night's light because suddenly Joan found herself in complete darkness. Chris gently placed her back against the rough wall, pinioned her there, and sought her mouth. He kissed her not just with his lips but with his whole being. Perhaps it was the roughness of the wall, but Joan was uncomfortable. Sensing this, Chris released her, regained his composure, and led her toward the lights of the house.

He told her their plans for Saturday, even though he had outlined them previously. He was about to say something else when the lights blinked three times. It was Mrs. Spriggins letting the girls know it was time to come in. Everyone recognized the signal, including Joan, thanks to Gloria, and began heading for the door. Chris gave Joan a gentle push in the direction of the door and said he would see her in the morning. Gloria was waiting in the lounge when Joan entered and together the two of them went to their room and had a long conversation about the party before falling off to sleep.

All Saturday Chris was the perfect host. Before and after the football game, he took her around campus and pointed out various buildings, facilities, and places of interest. He, too, gave her background information which included the story of William Wilberforce. She listened politely. But she was caught up by the sound of his voice and the animation in his green eyes. On a few occasions she had seen his eyes turn cold and cutting. Most of the time Joan loved looking at Chris. She adored his green eyes, and he seemed genuinely enthralled by her.

The All Students Dance later that evening gave Joan the chance to see how many others enjoyed the homecoming weekend. Her choice of dress, thanks to her mother's help, was exactly right. It was neither too childish nor too sophisticated. Both Gloria and Chris said how nice she looked.

Chris' good night that evening began as a repeat of Friday's parting. Chris led her to the alcove, but before they entered, Joan said, "I'd rather not."

"Please," he begged.

"Chris, you said that you would never ask me to handle what I couldn't or didn't want to. Were those just words?

"No, Joan. Those weren't just words. I meant them then and they still stand. It's just that —that I'm not used to being held in check. I suppose I really am my father's son." After a short pause, he continued. "You ought to know by now how right we are for each other. I wouldn't do anything to hurt you or to harm our future together, but I need you so badly and I need you now."

For a few moments, no one said anything. There was the sound of their breathing. Otherwise, the silence was unrelieved. When Joan made no move to give in to his entreaties, he took her hand and returned her to the sorority house. She could not read the look in his eyes when he said good night.

Sunday dawned bright and cold. Chris borrowed a friend's car to take her to the train station. They left the sorority house early enough to have breakfast before Joan's departure. Though they ordered a full meal, neither did more than pick at the food.

"Joan, thanks for a memorable weekend."

"Is that all it was, memorable?" she asked.

"No, it was more than that. I love you and I'm glad you're my girl. You're good for me, but in many ways we're quite different. In many ways you're still a child. I don't know how long I can wait for you to grow up."

"Chris, I love you, too, but there are certain things I just can't do. I'm not just thinking about what my parents would say. I know the kind of person I am and I don't think I'm a child because I won't do everything you want me to do."

"I'm trying to understand. But you need to try to understand me as well."

This was their first argument It was tiring. Finally they said they would miss each other terribly until Thanksgiving when the Williamses were scheduled to come to New Orleans. Chris took her to her train and gave her a quick kiss on the forehead. His hands stayed at his sides. By way of explanation he said, "I don't trust myself right now. Have a safe trip. I really am glad you came."

From her train window she watched as Chris faded into the distance. This time it was she who was leaving him.

Chapter 22

Joan was extremely tired when she arrived back in Chicago, but she did not regret her weekend. She had read somewhere that people often got more sleep than they required and that sleep could never be regained. Nevertheless, as soon as she got into her parents' car, she closed her eyes and went quickly to sleep. Being sympathetic to her needs, her folks let her go straight to bed once home until time for school, eager as they were to hear about the weekend. For them the particulars of the homecoming would have to wait.

Suzanna, however, could not wait. As soon as she saw Joan at school, she ran up to her and began pelting her with questions: "What was Wilberforce like? Did you really go to the Kappa House? Were all the guys as good looking as Chris? Did you tell him I said hello?"

Joan answered the questions briefly, as there was not much time between classes. She had to fudge a bit on the last one and said, "Of course, I didn't forget to give Chris a hello from you." Temporarily satisfied, Suzanna went off to class.

She made Joan promise to call her that afternoon with the unexpurgated version.

"Are you sure it's safe for me to divulge all of that over the phone?" Joan threw that last remark over her shoulder as she rushed to her next class.

At dinner that evening Joan went over the events of the weekend with her family and Suzanna. Rather than go through the whole thing twice, and in more detail than she cared to give, Suzanna was invited to have dinner with them. Betsy, of course, could always be counted on to ask the awkward question. Tonight was no exception.

"How many times did he kiss you?" she blurted out.

Joan passed over the question by continuing to describe the homecoming float that won first prize. Betsy knew that was a delaying tactic and repeated her question at the end of Joan's lengthy description.

"How many times did he kiss you?"

"Four," said Joan, supplying a random number.

"Oh, is that all? He's not such a hot sh-"

"That'll be enough, Betsy," said her father at last.

Joan could not resist adding, "It's the quality, not the quantity that's important."

By meal's end, everyone was satisfied with Joan's account of her weekend. Eventually, Betsy ran out of questions. She asked Joan some more about private aspects of her trip, but the answers she got were polite, if evasive. Kitty felt there was more to be learned, but decided that when the time was right, Joan would confide in her or Clarence.

There was little over a month before Joan would see Chris at Thanksgiving. She marked the days off on her calendar. About two weeks before they were to leave, Joan asked her mother to assist her once more with her wardrobe. Joan was a confident scholar. But selecting the right outfit still was not easy for her.

"Oh, Joan. I thought you knew. We're going to have to pass on Thanksgiving in New Orleans this year. We're going to D.C. instead."

"No, I didn't know. This is the first I've heard of it. I had planned to see Chris over the holidays. And I was so looking forward to meeting my grandparents."

"Joan, I'm really sorry. But this has been an unusual year. You've got to start getting some college applications out. You're already lagging behind in that area. I'm sure you'll get in somewhere good when they look at you records and the fact that you might skip your last year. A visit to Howard is a perfect start."

The two talked on, but Joan knew when she was defeated. There was no way she was going to change her mother's mind. She was sure that her father would also think a trip to Howard a necessity. So there was nothing to do but write Chris about the change in plans and arrange to see him over Christmas break. That done, she buried herself in her school work and hoped and even prayed that everything would work itself out so that she would see Chris after all for Thanksgiving.

This time, however, her prayers were not answered. All was going as her mother had planned. Chris had to spend Thanksgiving at home. He said he felt he owed it to his family since so much of the past summer had been spent away. He reminded Joan that they were putting him through college. He was not on scholarship and he was not employed. On top of that they were paying his fraternity bills as well as providing him with a more than liberal allowance.

"Joan, I'm really sorry about not seeing you. Believe me I am. But there's nothing I can do. I have to be with them for Thanksgiving. I hope you understand," he said when he called her one night.

Joan gave in to his way of thinking, but she was not happy about it. She wished him a happy holiday. She wanted to add that she was planning to be absolutely miserable. She restrained herself. She and Chris had never played with each other's emotions. She did not want to introduce that element into their relationship. It was tentative at best now. She did not want to give him an excuse to part with her.

The Thanksgiving holidays were not as bleak and miserable as Joan expected they would be. Her parents were excited about showing her their alma mater and the excitement was contagious. As the holiday was a brief one, only four days in all, they flew from Chicago's O'Hare Airport to Washington's National Airport. It snowed and the capitol was blanketed in soft whiteness. It was still and quiet. The effect was breathtaking. It was as though they had the city to themselves. Feeling the city was theirs, they set about enjoying it and Howard University. The campus was nearly deserted when the Williamses chose to visit it. Clarence and Kitty did not mind that. They were able to give Joan a personal tour with themselves as guides. Not only did they point out places of interest- the library, the administration building, the senior dormitory- but they reminisced about things that had happened almost two decades ago. Joan was as fascinated by their remembrances as she was by the tour.

Their last night in Washington, the Williamses dined at Gadsby's on Colonial Pastry and George Washington's Favorite Duck. For dessert they enjoyed Fudge Pye. The food was as delicious as ever, but this time Clarence and Kitty were able to have a good time. The last time they were here should have been like this. Even Betsy was happy. At first she was irked because the child's portion had been ordered for her. When she saw the size of the adult portions, she was content. On Sunday, the Williamses boarded a plane for the return trip.

Joan had a great deal to think about. Her folks were not pushing for a commitment, but she was positive that they wanted to hear how favorably Howard had impressed her. And it actually had.

But it was Wilberforce that had Chris and that was uppermost in her mind. So all she could tell her parents was that it was difficult to judge a school when the campus was deserted. She had seen Wilberforce at its best. She had felt its pulse. She had not seen Howard when it was full of life.

"After your explanation," Kitty said, "I understand, Joan."

"I hope you really do."

"Perhaps we could plan another trip."

"Time's running out for visiting schools, but I'll submit an application to Howard."

"Submit applications to both schools and see what happens."

"Good idea," said Joan, whose mind was already made up. She did not tell her mother that she had already applied to Wilberforce.

Chapter 23

The weeks until Christmas vacation dragged by. Suzanna persuaded Joan to attend a party, but the high point of these days was a long chat with Chris who had called her almost as soon as he arrived home for Christmas break. His college break began before Joan's.

"My folks are having a party tonight. There're so many people here that it'll be awhile before I'm missed," Chris said.

"My parents went out to a party. They'll be back shortly after midnight. I think they still feel funny about leaving Betsy and me alone."

"Yeah. They're funny, aren't they? They never really want to let go. But I didn't call to talk about parents. Baby, I miss you. I don't know how I got through Thanksgiving without you."

"Oh, I know. I know. I feel the same way."

"I just wish I could reach out and touch you right now. I want to feel myself in your embrace. It's lonely without you. I haven't been going out with anyone. My fraternity brothers have nick-named me 'The Monk.' It's been terribly lonely."

"Chris, if you needed to date someone, it'd have been okay."

"No, Joan. It wouldn't have been. I'm not looking for a substitute. It's you I want. I can hardly wait for you to be here. I tried to make that clear at Homecoming. I'm glad we'll see each other for Christmas."

The sudden switch from "baby" to her name made Joan pay attention. She listened very carefully as he continued opening up to her as he had only done once before. When the conversation ended, she realized the depth of his feelings. She wondered how she would be expected to respond when they next met in a few days time. She had not changed her mind about the kind of girl she was. She hoped he could wait for her. At the same time, she could barely wait to be with him again.

Christmas in New Orleans was a fairyland. Since the Williamses had to pass up the Thanksgiving reunion because of the college visit, it was decided that they would go to Louisiana for Christmas break. Kitty's mother and father warmly welcomed their son-in-law and their grandchildren. As usual they were overjoyed at seeing Kitty.

"Joan," said her grandmother with a French accent, "I've heard so much about you from La Verne, Chris' mother, that I feel I know you already. Come, ma petite, let me kiss you."

This was one of the few times that Joan had ever been favorably singled out when Betsy was around. Joan liked the warm feeling that came over her.

That first day she had to content herself with just a phone call from Chris. The DuPuis's were giving or attending dinners and parties almost every evening. It was the busiest social season of the year. Joan was included in everything and frequently Chris was at the same functions. Joan's days and nights were so organized that she and Chris had little time alone. When they did steal a few minutes of privacy, Chris reaffirmed his love but kept his ardor in check. It was a beautiful holiday, but as with all good things, it had to come to an end. Because Joan and Chris had not had much time alone together, the conversation begun in Ohio was not revisited. Everything seemed   settled.   They appeared to be girlfriend and boyfriend. Yet Joan had a feeling their relationship was not the way it used to be.

Returning to school after a vacation is a letdown for most. Joan's spirits were high because she could busy herself with her books and not take notice of the months that must pass until she would see Chris. Her parents were beginning to accept the idea that she might attend Wilberforce and only asked infrequently if she had news from Howard.

Late in January, Joan received a note saying that she needed to schedule an appointment with her guidance counselor. Joan hoped it was about her acceptance at Wilberforce or scholarship news. She knew she would not be eligible for much financial aid, but every little bit would help. Besides that, it would be good to see a scholarship listed for her on the graduation program.

Joan was ushered into the comfortable reception area of the senior guidance counselor and told to have a seat. She would be seen in a few moments. Joan relaxed in an overstuffed chair and looked at the view from the window. Traffic was light and a few snowflakes were whirling. The famous Chicago wind was blowing in full force. A real storm might be brewing. Before she could pursue this line of thought, Miss Thomas' student receptionist announced that Joan could now enter.

Joan said hello to Kim, who was just leaving the inner office, and then spoke to Miss Thomas. "I hope this is the news I've been waiting for about my scholarship or my admission to Wilberforce."

"Well, it is and it isn't."

"Oh, no," sighed Joan as she literally sank into the chair on the other side of Miss Thomas' desk.

"I certainly wouldn't view what I have to tell you in that light. You're a very competitive, young lady and you've received a full scholarship to..."

Joan could hardly believe her ears. A full scholarship! It was infinitely more than she had expected. "I'm so relieved. That's good-"

"Joan, it's more than good. It's wonderful," said Miss Thomas, trying to keep her annoyance from showing. "Now listen carefully this time. You did not hear everything I said before. You have been granted a four-year full academic scholarship to Vassar. Several prestigious Eastern colleges have been searching for academically talented minority women. I submitted your name and transcript to two or three and Vassar responded with the best offer. Now think of it! Do you know what this means?"

The counselor had much more to say and she droned on for what seemed like forever to Joan. Of course, Joan knew what it meant. It meant trouble. How would she be able to convince her parents to let her attend Wilberforce in light of this?

"Joan, you don't seem as excited as I thought. When I told Carol Lynn that the University of Illinois had accepted her, she could hardly contain herself. Yet when I tell you about Vassar, your mind seems elsewhere. Is something wrong?"

"No, nothing is wrong. I guess everyone responds to good news differently. I'm really very excited and nervous, too. I hadn't anticipated anything like this happening."

"But, Joan, that's what coming here was all about. Don't you remember our conversation a few years back? You were living on the west side then and I saw you at your home. We talked about preparing you for one of the best schools in the country. Well, you've certainly done your part, and now this is your reward."

Joan thought of it more as a cross than as a reward. However, what she said was, "My parents will be elated. Thanks for everything you've done to help. By the way, did you hear from any of the other schools I applied to?"

"Yes, you were accepted at all of them."

"Thanks again," said Joan as she put on what she hoped would pass for a sincere smile. Then she returned to class.

By the time school ended that day, word had spread about Joan's scholarship. Many of her classmates sought her out to shake her hand, pat her on the back, or simply say. "Great going." By the end of the day, Joan's spirits had risen also. She knew that never in a million years could she pass up this opportunity. No one in her right mind could ever think of turning down Vassar. Now she would just have to figure out how to tell Chris that she would not be joining him at Wilberforce in the fall.

The dinner table conversation at the Williams' household was extremely animated that night. Joan was the star and was brighter than ever. Even Betsy was awed into silence. So it was the "adults" who dominated the discussion. Joan's parents were more than excited. Electricity flowed. Their little girl had done it. She had received a reward for her hard work and recognition for her abilities in ways that counted. Vassar would be a door opener for Joan, who, no matter how bright, would still have to go on proving herself to the world. At least that task would be made easier by being a Vassar alumna.

After dinner, Joan, not Betsy, helped Kitty clear the dishes. Betsy did not argue about her chore being taken from her. She happily went off to watch television. When all the dishes were in the kitchen, Joan asked her mother, "Do you think this is the right decision? Vassar is going to be tough."

Kitty heard the question as Joan stated it, but she knew the question that was actually being asked. So she answered, "I think it would be wise if you called Chris tonight. He'll want to know your plans."

With that word from her mother, Joan headed for the telephone. On the way she looked in on Betsy and said, "Go help Mother with the dishes. They're ready to be washed."

Joan dialed the familiar number and waited while one of Chris' fraternity brothers went in search of him. A few moments later, Joan heard a friendly, "Hi, Joan. What's up? It's not even Saturday."

"I've got some news for you and it just couldn't wait until the weekend."

"Shoot."

"Vassar has awarded me a full scholarship," she blurted out.

"Joan, that's great, absolutely fantastic. I know you won't be coming here now. You've got an opportunity you can't turn down."

The rest of the conversation continued in that manner. By the time Joan hung up she was genuinely much happier. Everyone else, it seemed, knew what she was last to recognize. There could be no doubt about accepting the scholarship. She laughed aloud when she thought about how ridiculous she would look turning down Vassar.

Joan went back to the kitchen but found no one there except Betsy who was putting away the last of the dried dishes. "Mom's in the study," Betsy volunteered, reading Joan's mind.

The study door was ajar so Joan pushed it open without knocking and entered. She told her mother how excited Chris was for her.

"I thought that would be the case. He's a level-headed young man and knows the importance of taking advantage of opportunities."

"We still plan to see each other in April. He'd like to come here for spring break. I told him I didn't think you'd mind."

"No, I don't mind. But now that you two are dating, it'll be as your boyfriend, not simply as a house guest, that he'll be here."

"Mother, you don't have to worry about us. I know how to conduct myself and he does too. We'll be alright."

Kitty decided not to push the conversation at this point. The timing still was not right. There would be time to talk before Chris arrived. Instead Kitty directed their discussion to the purchases they would soon be making. There would be a typewriter and personal reference books. There would be a new set of luggage. Of course, there would be many new clothes. Kitty felt that looking good had a therapeutic effect. Looking good was something Kitty did amazingly well.

Chapter 24

"Joan, it's impossible. What will people think?" It was her dad's strong, firm voice speaking now.

"You really have put us in an awkward position. We know how fond you are of Chris, but a trip to New York alone is out of the question." It was Joan's mother's turn at moral indignation.

Several quiet weeks had passed since the acknowledgement by all that Joan would attend Vassar. As with most events around the Williams' house, that simply indicated the lull before the storm. The Williamses were not prepared for this type of shock. They knew that hard earned reputations could be shattered like delicate crystal.

"But look at it my way and put yourself in my situation," Joan entreated. "First, I'm more that just fond of Chris. I think I'm in love with him. He treats me like- like you used to, with respect and warmth and tenderness." *Well, he used to*, she thought. "Second, I've been brought up to know right from wrong. We don't need to go to New York to get into trouble. Third, it's vital to our relationship that he share this experience with me; I'll only see Vassar once for the first time. We'll need all of this to keep us going. I can't cut him out at a time like this."

"Joan, Joan, we do understand but-"

"Daddy, have you really given this enough thought? Have you really tried to feel about this the way I do? I don't want to do anything to hurt anyone. But I don't want to be hurt either and this is really very important to me."

"There'll be other young men," Kitty supplied at this point. "If Chris doesn't understand what Vassar means to you and if he can't brave the distance, then it wasn't meant to be."

"Mother, you can't believe what you're saying. The boys who wouldn't travel to my west side address haven't traveled to my Hyde Park address either. Only Bernie came around and he wasn't exactly received into your welcoming arms. Chris, to talk about distances, is willing to come from Ohio to spend not just his school vacation but his birthday as well. He cares about me; he's happy about my going to Vassar, but he needs something in return and -."

"Yes, Joan, I do see your point of view," her father interrupted. "But a trip alone is impossible. You know now that Chris is nearly legally an adult he'll have to be careful. You're still only sixteen - a minor." Her father meant this to be funny, but it was not received that way.

"Oh, my gosh! I'd never thought of that," cried Joan with real alarm.

Seeing the effect his words produced, her father tried to calm Joan. He was only minimally successful. At least he said no more about the impossibility of the trip to Vassar.

Joan returned to her room. Her eyes rested on the book she was reading for French class. Having done so well with one foreign language, she had added French to her studies. She was reading *Les Miserables*. *How apt*, she thought and cried herself to sleep.

Chris would be arriving in a few days. Nothing more was said about the New York trip, but Kitty did help Joan plan a birthday dinner for Chris. When he did arrive, everyone seemed truly happy to see him and to have him visit again.

The birthday dinner must have taken its toll on Chris because it was noon the day afterwards before he showed himself. Or maybe it was the wine he had drunk. Joan, however, had seen him take more than that during homecoming and it had not slowed him down.

"What happened to you?" Joan said, trying to be cheerful when he came into the living room.

"I didn't go to sleep right away. In fact, I went out for awhile."

"Oh, I didn't hear you leave- or return."

"I went to Old Town. It was sort of a last minute thought. I didn't really consider asking you because they sometimes check ID cards."

"Did you have a good time?" Joan asked, hoping her voice did not betray her hurt.

Apparently it did not because Chris continued to tell her about his night. Finally he got around to asking her if their trip to New York was on.

"No, it is not on. I'm not sure that I'll be able to convince them to let us go." With that she excused herself and returned to her room.

Suddenly her room felt oppressively small. *This is my house*, she thought. *Why should I be stuck in my room? Why am I acting as though everything depends on him? Obviously he has a separate existence. Why shouldn't I?* Thoughts such as these ran through her head. Unable to to stand it any longer, she picked up the phone and dialed Suzanna's number.

"Hi, Suzanna. This is Joan. Want to go out for an ice cream?"

"Sure. Just the two of us or is Chris coming?"

"Just the two of us," replied Joan.

"Oh! Is he sleeping it off? He put away a lot of beer last night."

"What? What did you say?"

"I said he put away a lot of beer last night."

"Where did you see him?"

Somewhat less sure of herself, Suzanna answered timidly, "He was at one of the spots in Old Town."

"Was he alone?" Joan hated herself the minute the question was out.

"Not for long he wasn't," replied Suzanna. "Hey, what about the ice cream? Can I meet you at the corner in half an hour?"

"Yes. I'll see you in thirty minutes."

Joan was already prepared to leave so she merely killed time until she left to meet her friend. It seemed to take forever for the minutes to tick by. At last she was on her way and she did not tell anyone where she was headed.

Her conversation with Suzanna was a real eye-opener. She was learning things about both of them that she never knew or was too blind to see.

"You've got him so wrapped up in you that he doesn't know which way is up," Suzanna said.

"You're exaggerating."

"No, I'm not. Listen. You're my friend, so I hope I can say these things without hurting you. You're a great friend; you're smart; you're nice; and you're pleasant to look at. But in that order. You're no raving beauty. Chris is about as handsome as they come. The other qualities that he may have are dwarfed by his looks. I've been told all my life how beautiful I am- peaches and cream complexion, chiseled features, long, dark silky hair, and hazel eyes," Suzanna said as if reciting items from a memorized list. "Yet I can't get Chris to pay attention to me- while he's sober. I saw him last night and I tried to see if I could-"

"Don't finish, Suzanna. I don't want to know."

"Oh, yes, you do. And if we're still going to be friends after this, you must know."

"Please, Suzanna, it really doesn't matter. Keep it to yourself. I don't want to hear any more." With that Joan stopped her ears with her fingers.

Suzanna reached across the table of the booth they occupied and tugged at Joan's arms. "Stop acting like a character from one of those books you're always reading. You must hear and you will hear." Worried that they were getting too loud, Joan reluctantly removed her fingers and listened to her friend.

Joan realized that she was about to learn how Chris had succumbed to Suzanna's feminine wiles. Suzanna shared with Joan how Chris turned the table on the seduction attempt without embarrassing either of them. He told Suzanna that both of them would regret anything done in haste and that he had too much to drink to put up much resistance. Rather than letting her continue with her plans, he excused himself and left the restaurant. At the end of the account, Suzanna asked Joan to forgive her for what she had tried. She explained that she had not meant anything personal by her actions but that the opportunity was there and she thought she would take advantage of it. She also asked Joan to tell Chris that she was sorry.

Joan felt it wiser to let Suzanna take care of that herself. She was not going to be a go-between for the two of them. She did, however, forgive her friend. In the future she asked her to find someone else to play around with.

"Suzanna, you were right, I really did want to know. But suppose this episode had an unhappy ending, unhappy for me that is. Please don't do anything like that ever again."

Now that Joan had spoken her final words on that subject, the two friends went on to enjoy the melted sundaes that remained in front of them. Joan was thinking that perhaps she had not jeopardized her chances with Chris. Maybe their relationship could be on her terms.

Chapter 25

When Joan returned home, she sought out Chris to apologize for her abrupt behavior. She was happy to see him smile at her peace gesture and even happier when he placed her face between his hands and kissed her forehead. She responded with a brief kiss on his lips and a promise to talk once again with her parents.

There was not much time remaining for Joan to convince her parents of the necessity of the visit as she had proposed it. Somehow she had to make them see it her way. Usually they were right, but about this she could not let them have the last word. Just before it was time for her mother to begin dinner preparations, Joan asked her parents to come into the kitchen for a few minutes. Clarence and Kitty were sure they knew what Joan wanted, but they agreed to come anyway.

"I'm sure you know why I asked you in here," Joan began with carefully measured words. "I will not bother you with this again. We must decide this now. I think you don't realize how vital this is to me. You've always treated me with love and respect. You have always done what's best for me. You've prepared me to live in a world where things do not come easily but must be fought for and jealously guarded. You've given me moral guidance. You have done a great deal for me, but haven't I done something good for you, too? No, don't answer now. Let me finish first," she said when she saw her mother about to say something. "You're proud of me because of my accomplishments. You enjoy sharing in my good fortune. Now continue to share with me, but also give me some independence. Let me start to stand on my own two feet. Please don't let the fact that I'm an intelligent female make me have to bear a double cross. As it is I will be tested all my life because of my dark color. But let me start to be responsible for that life."

There was total silence when Joan had finished her brief plea. Everything was at stake. They all knew what the unasked question was. They all knew an answer had to be given. They also knew that their future relationship hung on that response.

Their silence was so complete that all of the sounds that had gone unnoticed could now be heard. The faucet that had not been completely turned off dripped intermittently. The motor of the refrigerator revved up as more power surged through it. Even the almost inaudible buzz from the electric clock that hung on the kitchen wall could be clearly heard. Suddenly a shrill cry sounded. The tea kettle that Joan had put on the stove was whistling violently.

"Oh, I'd forgotten I was fixing water for coffee. I thought you and Dad might enjoy some while discussing your answer."

Seeing that an answer was expected forthwith, Joan's parents prepared their coffee and sat down to talk about what Joan had said. A slight breeze was playing gently with the tree tops that were just beginning to show spring buds. The still bright sun bathed the kitchen with its warmth. There the Williamses sat and debated what they would say to Joan. In the meantime, Joan and Chris decided to take a walk in the neighborhood. They felt the need for physical activity while Kitty and Clarence talked. Betsy, sensing that she should be out of the way, went to visit a friend and managed to get herself invited to dinner as well.

When it was time to eat at the Williams' house, it was just Kitty, Clarence, Joan, and Chris. Kitty knew that now was a good time to clear the air. Never having been one to miss an opportunity herself, she started in as soon as the dinner prayer was finished.

"I know you're anxious to hear what's been decided." Kitty's glance encompassed Joan as well as Chris. "But first let me say that we are proud of you and do share in all of your good fortune...." Kitty went on in that vein for several minutes before getting to the point that really interested her audience. Get there she eventually did.

"Your father and I think it would be a good idea for us all to see Vassar and make a final commitment once that's been done. We've checked train schedules and can leave tomorrow morning. We can visit the school and take in a play before returning to Chicago. The trip and the play will be our belated birthday gift to Chris. We'll rent a car while we're there and you and Chris can drive in together to see Vassar. Later perhaps the two of you will give us the grand tour of the campus."

Joan had not missed a single word her mother had said. Even though Kitty was trying to make all of this sound like her idea, Joan realized she had won. It was an important victory for her because she and her mother were rarely at odds over really serious issues. They approached things differently, it was true. But it was with what was best for the family that was uppermost in their minds. This victory gave Joan an insight into how her mother had operated all of these years. It was not from selfishness. With this suddenly clear, Joan rushed from her seat, dropping her napkin as she did, ran over to her mother, and threw her arms around her neck.

"Mother, I love you so much," she said unashamedly.

Chris interrupted this family scene with a reflection of his own. "I wish my parents were as responsive to my needs as you and Uncle Clarence are to Joan's. But they listen to whatever my sister has to say as though the high and mighty had spoken."

"Chris, I didn't know you have a sister," Joan said truly surprised. "I don't recall meeting her when we were in New Orleans for Christmas."

"At my house you wouldn't know that she has a brother," Chris announced with an undisguised note of bitterness in his voice. "But let's not dwell on that. If we're leaving tomorrow, I'd better start packing."

As soon as the meal was completed, everyone began in earnest to get ready for the trip. Betsy was informed of the plans but said she did not want to go. It was arranged for her to remain at her friend's for the few days her own family would be gone. The downstairs neighbors agreed to take in the mail and the papers. Everyone retired earlier than usual, satisfied that a happy and mutually agreeable solution had been reached.

Before Kitty turned out the lamp by her nightstand, she somewhat jokingly told her husband that she would have to do without the new clothes she had planned to buy. This trip was going to eat into that extra money. Clarence assured her that she always looked great to him and they soon fell asleep in each other's arms.

Joan, too, was falling asleep in Chris' arms. They had decided at the last minute to watch the late night movie on television. The excitement and tension of the day registered and long before the movie was over, Joan was sound asleep, cradled in Chris' arms.

The train ride was relaxing. Nevertheless, there was an earnestness about the trip that made itself felt. As one landscape fused with the next, Joan and Chris' conversation crossed topics. Both knew this was a turning point and they crowded as many thoughts in as they possibly could. Kitty and Clarence were caught up in a rather quiet introspection. They held hands, smiled occasionally, and nodded as if in agreement with some internal question. They arrived in New York City, went directly to their hotel rooms, and sunk into a deep, dreamless sleep. Refreshed by their rest, they decided not to waste the evening. Chris was allowed to select the play he would like to see, and after dinner they all took in a light musical comedy.

The following morning was a bright, clear one. Joan and Chris wanted to get an early start despite their late night out. Clarence had arranged for a rental car and it was now at the hotel. In the lobby, Chris studied the map to discover the best route to take them to Poughkeepsie.

"Drive carefully," cautioned Joan's father.

"I will." With that Joan and Chris were out of the hotel lobby.

Chris handled the rental Chevrolet easily. He seemed to have a natural affinity for mechanical things as well as for human beings. Before long he eased the car onto Route 55 which eventually led them to Raymond Avenue. They enjoyed the scenery, talked about whatever entered their minds, and alternately listened to the radio. About a mile farther, after reaching Raymond Avenue, they came to a stone archway that was the main entrance to Vassar.

"Would you like to take a picture of the archway? It's a marvelous architectural structure, isn't it?" said Chris, not expecting disagreement.

"I'll take the picture, but I want you in it. I don't have a single one of you."

They took their photos. Joan took one of him and he likewise took one of her in the archway. Each knew what the other was thinking, but neither made a comment.

Once inside Joan and Chris were awed by the sight of the flowers in front of Vassar's main building. A ring of lily-flowering tulips was blooming in the 120-foot circumference of the circle of the building.

"First the impressive stone and now the flowers," Joan said. "I know I could like it here."

Deciding to walk around the campus rather than drive, the two strolled hand in hand. They took slow, careful steps. Joan commented on everything and on each building she saw. She shared with her companion the feeling she had when first viewing Hyde Park High. Walking like this with Chris made her totally open and reflective. Chris was an attentive listener. He did not say much, but a knowing look and a squeeze of the hand at the appropriate times were all Joan needed. After more walking and "talking," Joan asked Chris what he thought of it all.

At first he talked about the buildings. He especially raved about the Gothic-style Frederick Ferris Thompson Memorial Library which dated back to 1905. Then he went on to talk about what was really important to the two of them.

"Joan, I know this is what you want. And I think it's right for you. All I can add is that I'm glad that you're my girl and the distance won't make any difference."

"Chris, it is what I want, but I don't want it now. Remember when you said I was still a child? In some ways I guess you were right, but I didn't see it then. I don't want to miss my senior year. There's so much I could never recover. I don't want to leave home yet. I thought I was ready, but I'm not. I don't know exactly why I feel this way. There are so many questions that I don't have answers to. Perhaps when I grow up I'll understand, or at least I hope I will."

Chris nodded as though he did understand. There was not much he could add, so he opted for silence. Together they strolled back to the car, his arm was around her shoulder and her arm was around his waist. They both took another look as the view of the campus receded.

Breaking the silence, he asked, "Are you ready to share this with your folks?"

"Yes. I'm ready. They're adults. They'll understand."